The Alphabet of Dating

Also by Joseph Anthony

An Uneaten Breakfast: Collected Stories and Poems

"Warm poetry and short stories make a pleasant combination. Captivating—keeps the reader on the edge of his or her chair." –Bea Smith, The Local Source

"Using lyrical poetry and prose, Mr. Anthony adeptly weaves a map of the emotional landscapes within and between his characters. *An Uneaten Breakfast* resides strongly and comfortably among classic and contemporary masterpieces." –Samsara Literary Magazine

Praise for *The Alphabet of Dating*

"Will have you cataloging your own quest for love. Seasoned, crisp…and full of universal truths." –Richard Polk, author of *Mantis Prayers* and *The Boarder on Monroe Street*

"An intriguing tale of the nuance of relationships and the impact they have on us all." –Linda Rawlins, author of *Sacred Gold* and *Fatal Breach*.

Diamond Mill Press

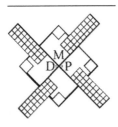

Debbie,

2021

The Alphabet of Dating

Joseph Anthony

Thanks for Reading!

Best Wishes!

Joseph Anthony

Published by Diamond Mill Press
184 South Livingston Avenue Suite 9-198
Livingston, NJ 07039
www.diamondmillpress.com
facebook.com/diamondmillpress

The Alphabet of Dating

Follow Joseph Anthony on Twitter & Instagram:
@AuthorJ_Anthony

ISBN # 978-0-9838745-8-4

Library of Congress Control Number: 2015939966

10 9 8 7 6 5 4 3 2

Cover design by Anthony Prasa and Joseph Anthony
Cover photo (chalkboard) by Joseph Anthony
Cover photo (heart) © Rangizzz | Dreamstime.com, with permission
Author photograph by Linda Belardo

For my parents, who got it right.

And for all of the letters in my alphabet.

The Alphabet of Dating

AA

Everything feels so right when I think about your initials. *AA*. There is no one who could have come first. Whenever I was in the throes of another bad relationship, I would wonder what it might have been like, the two of us. Could my alphabet really have been that short? You were the first person to express interest in me. I remember how terrified I was when my mom came home from her PTA meeting and told me that she had been talking to your mom, had found out that you had a crush on me. That was all she said. When we are young we rely on our mothers to do our bidding, but the rest gets left up to us at some point.

In the margins of my notebooks I scrawled our initials over and over to see how they would fit. Then, I would steal peaks over your shoulder to see if you were doing the same.

We were fifth graders, ten-year-olds.

I never asked you out because I was a scared little boy, intimidated by you, and not yet comfortable in my own skin. We went through grade school seeing each other in the occasional classes we shared, and I couldn't help feeling closer to you than we really were.

It always made me a little sad to see you, to think about what we might have missed out on.

How have you been?

AB

It's so hard to recover from a disappointing first impression. A random bit of unfortunate luck ruined your chance from the start.

Traffic had kept you from getting to the Starbucks on time, but that wasn't it.

You had texted me to let me know that you were running late, that you would be there at 6:15 instead of 6:00. So I took a seat in an armchair by the window and people-watched while I waited.

No free parking spots made you more than fifteen minutes late, but that wasn't it either.

Your unfortunate luck occurred at precisely 6:23, when someone who looked an awful lot like you walked into the café a few minutes after you said you would be there.

AB

It wasn't just that this person walked into Starbucks looking a lot like you. This person came in, sat down at the first available table without ordering, and began texting.

I looked down at my phone and waited for it to buzz.

Nothing.

So I went back to your dating profile and compared the person texting at the table by the door against your pictures. It took a moment, but it was clear that I was more attracted to this new person than I was to you. Two minutes later, you walked in looking like a duller, less shiny version of the person I had mistaken for you.

Maybe the moral of the story is to make sure to be on time. Or perhaps it's just a simple reminder that luck always plays its part.

AB

And yet, you still had a chance.

    We ordered our drinks, crossed the street, and headed for the park outside. The bench we chose to sit on had a clear view of the playground, and I commented that there were a lot of kids running around.

    "I hate kids," you said.

    I have always loved kids.

AB

I'll admit, it impressed me when you mentioned you had a pilot's license.

At the end of the date, however, when you told me to text you later as we hugged goodbye, I said I would, knowing I wouldn't.

AH

If I had been you I never would have trusted me.

You knew nothing about me and yet there you were.

Telling me where your house was.

Getting into my car.

Coming back to my apartment.

Resting your head on my shoulder as we watched television until we both felt like enough time had passed so that we could touch each other without feeling dirty about what we were doing.

"I'll do anything you want me to do," you told me.

A little thrown, I pulled my head back, reconsidered what I was doing.

We ended up having fun, but not nearly as much fun as we could have had. Sometimes, when I'm feeling lonely—in desperate need of human contact—I think back to that moment and wish that I wasn't such a nice guy.

AH

"I'm sorry," I said. "I just can't get comfortable."

My tossing and turning was keeping you awake. It can be difficult trying to fall asleep in the same bed as someone else when you aren't used to sleeping with other people.

"It's fine," you said.

So we tried a little longer, but eventually I decided to sleep on the couch.

The next morning, when I asked if you had slept well, you said, "No, not so good."

That surprised me because I had slept like a baby, at least for a few hours. Maybe it's not the tossing and turning of the other person that keeps us awake at night, maybe it's how out of place we feel in a bed that isn't our own.

AH

Twenty minutes later, we were back outside your house. You lingered in my car, waiting for me to say that I would call you. Or perhaps, you were trying to come up with a reason of your own as to why we should just leave the night for what it was and both move on. You walked up the front steps and emptiness fell over the car. Not a sad loneliness but the welcomed relief of solitude. I drove away, certain I would never see you again.

B

BR

You were the one I told my mother I was dating when I wasn't. You ran in the popular-kid circle, just outside of my almost-popular-kid circle.

"Are you seeing anyone?"

"No, Mom."

"Why not? I don't want you to end up like Uncle Raymond."

"I'm not going to end up like Uncle Raymond."

"You're in high school now. You should be dating. Is that what you want? To end up alone?"

After months of this, she wore me down.

Eventually when she asked, I said: "Yes," and threw out your name.

BR

From then on, I no longer had to hear *Are you seeing anyone?* but your name led to a whole mess of other questions.

Of course, I felt guilty. There were no notebooks with your initials scribbled next to mine. I told her what little I knew about you, filling in the missing pieces with my imagination.

BR

Beneath my bed there is a shoebox with a teddy bear in it, because my mother insisted that I buy you a souvenir on our spring vacation. So reluctantly, I picked out a stuffed bear wearing a rainbow tie-dye shirt, and paid for it with money I had earned mowing lawns the previous summer. Our first day back at school, after the break was over, I told her that I had given it to you and that you loved it.

She had no reason to believe otherwise.

Don't ask me why but I've kept it all these years, found myself unable to throw it away. It's so old, yet still brand new. A silent symbol of something that never was.

BR

When I got tired of pretending, when I was more worn down by the questions than ever, I had you break up with me.

If anyone ever asks, it was because you *no longer felt the same way about me.*

That afternoon, after school, I feigned depression as best I could, kept my head down and tried to think about the dog we had to put to sleep when I was seven years old.

"Do you want to go out in the street and play catch?" my dad asked—imagining, I'll bet, that he was helping me through something monumental in my life.

That was my first break up.

C

CD

It was a silly thing to do, looking back, but all I had to go on was that you liked manga art and tennis. And since I had no idea as to what manga art was, I chose tennis even though I'd never played before.

```
Me: We should play tennis
You: Okay when?
Me: At the park...Tomorrow night if ur
     free?
You: That could work
Me: Is seven good?
You: Should be, but I've got to warn you,
     I'm pretty good
```

As soon as we stopped texting, I jumped in the car and headed to the mall, where I bought a cheap racket—on clearance, because I wasn't sure how long you would last. Later the next night, as you pulled into the park, I was still pulling the shrink wrap off the handle as you killed the engine.

Your headband said you meant business.

Your game, however, was lacking.

I won the first two games easily, carried you the rest of the way by sending balls into the net and claiming that you had more stamina than me. It clearly meant more to you, and although I wanted to win, losing seemed like a necessary sacrifice.

It went all the way to love.

"Forty-Love," you called out the score.

That's where I started trying. I fought back to tie it. Made you say, "Deuce."

Your serve.

No ace up your sleeve.

I returned it—relying on you to get the ball back to my side of the court before I could send it long and give you the deciding game.

But you spiked it. Sent it by me before I had the chance to throw the last point.

Afterward, while we sat cross-legged with our backs against the chain-link fence, sipping Gatorade, you said, "I think you let me win."

I argued, but only a little.

CD

The plan was to the head to 7-Eleven to buy Slurpees before walking around the park. It was the perfect autumn night, just before the clocks fell back and the trees got naked.

"So how long did you say you've lived in town?"

"I moved here about a month ago, don't know many people. I have one friend who has been trying to show me around. He and I went to the zoo today and I rode the flying fox."

Even though I wanted to ask about your friend, who he was, how you knew him, I knew it was too soon. "Have you ever seen the skyline?"

"No."

At the next light I made a left, swung up the S-turns that headed toward the reservation.

I still owe you that Slurpee.

CD

The South Orange reservation is home to night joggers, whitetail deer, and people hooking up in cars under the discretion of darkness. Even the police turn a blind eye because who wants to see all that? You can park your car near the woods, walk up onto a platform that stands above a valley, God knows how many feet below, and only a small stone wall separates you from the plunge. There are trees in this valley, tall and proud with branches that hide the skyline in the spring and summer, reluctantly reveal pieces of it in autumn, and proudly show it through their bare sticks in the cold winter months.

"Shit. There's still too many leaves on the trees," I said. "You can usually see all of the buildings perfectly."

"No, this is still amazing."

"Somewhere over there is the Empire State Building." I gestured toward the left, pointed at the treetops, cursing them to myself. "There it is! No, wait. That's the Chrysler building."

"Cool," you said, expectantly, guessing what my plan was.

Just then, headlights lit up the gravel road, a car pulled up, parked by a picnic table, and from it limped an old man with a cane.

Foiled.

"On September 11th, my sister and I came here with our mom and we could see the black smoke rising up into the sky."

You were half impressed, half disappointed that I hadn't made a move sooner. Even in the dark, disappointment is visible on a face.

"Let's go get that Slurpee."

We made our way back to the car.

CD

As I was driving toward 7-Eleven, I remembered something, pulled down a dead-end side street at the top of a hill that stood a few hundred feet higher than the reservation.

"I'm kidnapping you."

I put the car in park, we both got out, and I pointed back at the New York City skyline, now visible off and on between the houses on the street.

"Whoa," your mouth fell open.

I don't remember my first time looking at it—it is confounding, the splendid things we take for granted because we are so close to them, how when things are far away we seem to appreciate them more. I trust that you will always remember your first time, and, if I'm lucky, you will maybe think of me.

"You can see the way the world curves!" you said, and I knew the sight wasn't lost on you. "This is utterly amazing."

That's when I made my move.

CD

You can tell so much from a kiss.

Your lips were soft. Your mouth was gentle, confident, and precise.

You didn't force-feed me your tongue like so many others. In fact, you were shy about giving it. When I pulled away, I said, "I wonder how often the people in these houses see this going on."

"Probably all the time."

"'Meryl, it's happening again! We have got to move away from all this kissing,'" I joked.

"'Oh no, Mort…not again,'" you added.

"Hey, there's the Freedom Tower." I pointed at the tall, square-shaped building.

You called me a romantic, eyes cast toward the infinite lights.

CD

When we went back to the park, to pick up your car, the place was deserted. Had it been a movie, we would have seen tumbleweeds blowing by beneath the glow of the orange streetlights. The basketball courts, tennis courts, street hockey rink, racquetball courts, were all empty. Ghosts of athletes past watched us walk up the path toward the playground.

A 737 roared overhead, shook us the way fireworks give you that *pop* feeling in your throat.

"There must be an airport close by," you said.

I was more concerned with the man walking towards us, his little terrier on a leash. He gave us a nod, I waited until he got a hundred feet away before kissing you again.

"I've got one more surprise for you."

"Swings!"

We started off separately, each with our own feet dangling, scraping the dirt while we swung. Until you jumped off, landed gracefully, waited for me to slow down before jumping onto my lap and wrapping your legs around me.

We stayed like this for almost an hour. Lip-locked beneath a navy, star-soaked sky. As my pants grew tighter, I knew you could feel it, and I felt the need to say something.

"I don't know if you were expecting anything more from tonight but…" I'm not the kind of person who sleeps with someone early on if I really like them.

"What? Oh, no. I'm fine with just kissing."

"I'm sorry I ruined the mood."

"No," you said. "You didn't."

But it felt like I had.

Resting your head on my shoulder, I laced my fingers together in the small of your back. An end to the night was inevitable. We hadn't taken more than two steps back toward our cars when you slid your hand into mine and held it. It caught me off guard, made me shudder inside. I was so grateful for this gesture.

Up until then, I had always been the one who initiated that sort of thing. I couldn't bring myself to tell you that you were the first person to ever take *my* hand first. How would that have sounded?

It's always nice to take someone's hand and have them allow you to hold it. But to receive someone's, without having to ask for it, is physical proof that they want to hold your hand. That they want to be closer to you.

"Let's go back to the tennis courts," I insisted.

You didn't argue, but your look said *this is already longer than I intended to stay out tonight, so don't push it.*

CD

After stepping back between the lines on the court, I pressed my lips against yours, this time harder—more desperately than on the swings. The heat made our foreheads stick together. You slid your hands into my back pockets and we swayed there listening to the wind in the trees.

The night had come full circle.

CD

Later, just as I had gotten out of the shower and was getting
ready for bed, you texted me.

> You: I had a wonderful time tonight... Thank
>   you for everything

I tried to play it cool, took my time brushing my teeth
before answering.

> Me: Me too :) I can' t wait to see u again
> You: You really are a romantic
> Me: How about that skyline? :D

I climbed into bed knowing that I would either fall fast
asleep or not sleep at all.

CD

Secretly, I had more selfish reasons for kissing you on the tennis courts.

Yes, I was bringing the night full circle, but what I really wanted was to be able to walk by whenever I visited the park and conjure up the image of us.

CD

"Take a picture for me." By then you had opened up to me, shown me some of your photography, and in return I showed you some of my poetry.

"What do you want me to take a picture of?"

What I really wanted to ask for were pictures of things that made you think of me. To see how you saw me through your own eyes. But I was too afraid to ask, too scared of what I might see. So instead I asked for "Two people playing tennis."

"How about a picture of two people holding hands?"

"I'd love that."

"It's settled then. I'll know the right hands when I see them."

A week later you found them. We were out to dinner on a double date with my brother and his fiancé.

"Would you all excuse me for a moment," you asked, winking at me. Instead of heading for the restroom you went back to the car and grabbed your camera. After dinner, on our way out of the restaurant, I held the door open for everyone as we left, and you lingered behind, camera ready.

Their fingers laced in the parking lot. We had our picture.

CD

Danger.

Full speed ahead.

It feels so good to get lost in the other person. Where each new thing you learn is like opening a tiny present. Going that fast can make you lose sight of yourself. Things that usually matter—school, your job, friendships, calling your mother—all take a back seat while you're riding shotgun on a ride you can influence but never fully control.

Because there is another person involved.

While you're falling that hard, it's so easy to forget that each of you only has one hand on the wheel, and you may crash at any moment.

CD

There are so many questions I will never have the answers to.

What changed?

What could I have done differently?

Was there something wrong with me?

It happened on the highway, where we went to feel a rush and alive. I had dared you to run across from one side to the other.

"Easy," you said. "Piece of cake."

The danger, after all, was only in our heads—trickery born in our own minds, nature's way of keeping us from taking risks we should not take if we do not wish to get hurt.

It was after midnight and the cars were sparse. They could be seen approaching in either direction from half a mile off. "Alright then," I said, reaching for your fingers out on the shoulder of route 280.

But you wouldn't give them to me.

Instead you pulled your arm away and took off running.

CD

All of the important things seem to come three or four words at a time.

> I like you.
> I like you, too.
> We should go out.
> You're smothering me.
> I need some space.
> Where were you?
> You make me happy.
> Let's take a break.
> It's me, not you.
> Let's move in together.
> I love you.
> I don't love you.
> Let's start a family.
> I really love you.
> Will you marry me?
> Yes, I'll marry you.
> Okay, it's you.
> I cheated on you.
> I never loved you.
> You're breaking my heart.
> Let's still be friends.
> I'll always love you.
> I miss you.

So when you said, "We need to talk," I sat there with my elbow on my knee and my forehead in my palm, waiting for the four words I knew were coming next: "I've met someone else."

CR

There are a lucky few with short alphabets. But for most people it's an expensive, painful struggle.

It cost me twelve dollars for miniature golf, and I knew by the fourth hole that things would not work out. You hadn't said two words to me since I picked you up. We played speed golf, racing through the holes, all eighteen of them in twenty-two minutes.

"I've never played this fast before," you said, and for a moment I felt reckless for rushing things away.

There were so many wasted dollars.

So much wasted time.

A big part of my heart and faith in people—wasted.

If I end up at twenty-six letters or a hundred letters, the ride will at least have been something.

D

DL

Just once, I tried to have a long-distance relationship. The space between Chicago and New Jersey is well over 700 miles, but it certainly didn't feel like that far whenever we talked online or over the phone.

This is the magical thing about connections: they can shrink distances, fold maps, and wipe out oceans.

DL

Sometimes when I'm alone in my car, I think about how we used to listen to the radio over the phone together. Alternating between your music and mine, until your music began to feel like my music.

Taking turns listening over speaker-phone, until late past midnight, when one of us would fall asleep, leaving the other to ask: "Hey, are you still there?"

"Are you still…there?"

Over and over.

DL

A month in, you said, "Don't freak out, but I think I love you."

My response to this, as is often the case, changed everything.

"Really?"

There you were out on a limb, not sure about your feelings, unsure if what we had was virtual or real, but at least you had been brave enough to say it. I felt something too—albeit, not full-blown manic love—but I never even offered you a cliché, a lifeline of *And I love talking with you, too.*

A week later you told me that you had begun seeing someone in the town next to yours, and it became clear that at least part of the connection has to be physical.

E

EB

"Would you like to maybe grab coffee or see a movie with me sometime?"

"I think you're really sweet, but you just aren't my type."

F

FD

Kissing in a swimming pool—noodles under our arms as we put our hands on each other's backs to keep from drifting apart. The sun was setting, and the horses came out of the barn to look at the purple sky and chew at the grass, as the heat evaporated from the day. I've always loved the taste of chlorine, and it was even better off your lips. Our feet dangled in the deep end as our toes launched us off the slanted floor, only the noodles could save us from drowning. Soon your lips got really cold, and I realized that I was really cold. All light had vanished.

FD

Shivering, we dried ourselves off with the thin towels that soak through too fast.

"Who would buy these?" you asked.

"I don't know. I'm just house-sitting while my neighbors are away."

You sipped your beer and I tried to make out the tattoo on your leg through the darkness.

"Do you like country music?"

"Sure. I think most people are starting to come around. To open up their minds a little."

I pressed a button and the patio's surround sound clicked on. Cowboys serenaded us while we leaned back on our pool chairs to stare at the stars. From there, we talked about school and the future.

FD

We fell out of touch. Drifted apart, anyway.

FS

Ten p.m. felt a little late for a first date but that's when the special started.

"Applebee's is my favorite," you beamed in the parking lot lights as we approached.

The waiter came over, alerting us to what we already knew. Half-price appetizers was the reason we were there.

"There is also a beer special," he said. "Domestic pints for two-fifty and craft beers for four-fifty."

You slid your fingers across the glossy menu, waited for me to order, as if that would tell you something vital about me.

"I'll have a Blue Moon."

At first I thought I had made a mistake.

"Do you have anything pumpkin flavored?" you asked.

"I'm sorry, no."

Then you slammed the menu shut. "Okay, make it two Blue Moons." And I knew we at least had a chance.

FS

You: How was work?

Me: Work was tiring... Just getting put now

You: Put?

Me: Sry... Out*

You: Ur just getting out now? Isn't it
     kinda late to still be teaching?

Me: Yes... But I had an eye doctor's appt.
    After school ended

It was your inability to trust me that sunk us so quickly. I wasn't ready to tell you the truth. That your new boyfriend enjoyed going, once a month, to talk about his problems with someone who was paid to listen.

Embarrassment wasn't the reason I held that back, some things I just chose to play close to the vest early on. We didn't last long enough for me to tell you that whenever I said I was at the eye doctor, I was really somewhere else.

FS

It was the fifth of July. The children—still high on fireworks—reveled at the park down the street from my place, where we sat on the front steps eating Firecracker popsicles.

"You've hardly said two words all day," you reminded me, as if this was some secret you could no longer keep.

I bit the red top of the Firecracker off and chewed it all at once, thinking of him—how he always loved to eat ice chips when it was hot out.

"You're shutting me out. I really can't take this, how you're open one minute and so closed off the next."

Biting the sides like corn-on-the-cob, I mixed the cool white flavor with the blue, let the ice pop fall to the stoop where in melted like butter on a frying pan.

"What the fuck is wrong with you?" you demanded.

Finally, I turned toward you. "Today would have been my brother's birthday."

FS

Sometimes, I grouped the same excuse too close together. After my appointment, I came over to your place for dinner and to watch a sitcom on TV. As soon as the program cut to its first commercial, you turned, squinted at me hard and said, "Something must be wrong with your eyes."

FS

When I really went to the eye doctor, I said I was going to the dentist.

G

G

The waitress extended her sympathy, "We see this all the time."

I had been sitting there for half an hour, wearing my green collared shirt, just like I said I would be.

"Don't feel bad, it happens more often than you might think."

I ordered a rum and coke.

"On the house," she said, setting it down in front of me.

It would be cute if I said, "Your loss." If I pretended that it didn't bother me one bit.

But it did.

At least for a day, I thought of you, whoever you are. How I had gone to that restaurant relying on good faith, knowing little more about you than your first name and that you preferred kittens to puppies. As I drank, I debated whether or not to delete my online dating profile.

I flipped a coin.

Put down a ten-dollar bill and left.

H

HB

Skin on skin.

Dizzy.

"This will only be for tonight."

"Fine with me."

We contribute against our own cause.

Drink.

"Take your belt off."

"It shouldn't be this difficult."

"You've got that right."

It should not be this difficult.

HN

That moment when you see an attractive person in the supermarket and they actually start flirting with you.

You're thinking *this is too good to be true.*

And then they say, "You don't remember me, do you?"

HN

"How've you been?" you asked.

"Pretty well. Yourself?"

You could have been anyone. After enough failure, people begin to blend together. A smirk indicated that you were enjoying this—making me squirm.

Who were you?

What had I done to you?

Even though I always had good intentions, it often all turned to shit, anyway.

Doing right by people isn't easy.

"You're a teacher, right? We met online," you reminded me. "We talked for a week. Then you disappeared."

"I'm sorry."

You shook your head. "I'm not mad. It's just funny running into you. I'd know your face anywhere. I was excited about you."

HN

Sharing a bagel with pigeons in Madison Square Park it occurs to me. I, too, am letters in an alphabet.

HN

One month my subscription ended and I didn't bother to renew it. I had met people online that wanted me to delete my account after the first date so that "It could be just us," and I cannot imagine a worse demand to make.

That sentiment has to be mutual. A good first date does not mean the beginning of a relationship. To force it right away is to clip a bird's wings before it has even considered if it wants to fly.

The company sent me an email the next month telling me that I should consider coming back to their website if I hadn't yet found the right person.

"We do, after all, have over five-million members to browse through."

As if to mock me, the email contained my profile picture and the first few lines of my "About Me" section. This was their way of telling me that my account was something they still had control of. It must have slipped my mind to clear out the old messages. I had forgotten to delete my pictures, erase my self-description, and my lists of favorite movies, books, and bands.

Blank it.

Only instead of covering things up I would have been stripping them away.

As far as I know that profile remains somewhere in a cloud, a perfectly preserved virtual version of me that can still be seen. With an inbox full of messages that will forever go unanswered:

- Hey, i like your profile. We should get coffee sometime :)
- OMG! I like puppies too!
- We have so much in common, hmu
- wanna fuck?
- u there?
- You seem really cool, we live close by. Let me know if you want to hang out
- I'm excited about you
- Got any more pics?
- why aren't you answering?
- ...just say if ur not interested..
- HELLO?! Are you there?
- Are u still...there??

I

Me.

And only me.

Like all of those nights when I went to bed alone. Like the days that made up the spaces between dates, between relationships. Whenever there was no "You," and no "We," there was still me.

I always had I.

J

JC

You had been my best friend since kindergarten. And while you kissed me on the cheek during a romantic movie when we were eleven years old, I never realized just how much you must have liked me all of those years growing up.

Until one night in my basement when everyone else had gone home after a party. We were sitting on the couch next to each other, both really drunk, and you tried to kiss me. Even intoxicated I knew that it was something I did not want to have happen. I pulled my head back, gave you my neck, and I was thankful when your lips missed mine.

JF

On most days I would have said that you weren't my type. It was hot out, though, and I could have gone for an iced tea anyway. Main Street in Millburn can be a pleasant walk for a first date, we were off to a good start. And then you spent the next forty-five minutes talking about yourself, and I knew there would not be a second date.

JF

When you said, "I hope to see you again."
    And I said, "This was a nice walk."
    What I really wanted to say was, "No way in hell."

JG

I used to see you out running on the street around the corner from my old apartment every morning on my way to work. When I finally built up the courage to pull over to the side of the road to talk to you, I asked, "What's the easiest way to get to Columbia Turnpike?"

You pulled the headphones out of your ears, approached the car while I repeated the question. "You're headed straight for it. Keep going straight and you'll hit it. Then it's a left or a right depending on which way you're going."

"Thanks, I'm from a few towns over, not too familiar with this area. Know anywhere good to eat?"

"There's a waffle house down the hill in the valley, right next to the train station. You'll need to turn left when you get to the Turnpike." You bent down, untied and retied your sneaker.

"Sometimes I go there in the middle of a run. Kind of defeats the purpose, but once in a while it's okay to have a little fun."

You licked your lips.

I thanked you and pulled away. Found the waffle house right where you said it would be when I went looking for breakfast the next morning. Every Saturday and Sunday morning for a month I went there, waiting for you to walk in. I'm convinced that the staff thought I was crazy, some waffle loving fiend destined for diabetes from all the sugary syrup. Finally, just as I was about to give up, you came in.

The booth I had been sitting at faced the door, there was no way you could miss me as you entered. I waved. You smiled as you wrapped the wire of your headphones around your iPhone. "Hey, I remember you, glad to see you found the place."

You sat down across from me, ordered for the both of us, ran your foot up my leg while we ate. I gave you my number and we made plans to see each other again.

JG

Dedicated.

    Wistful.

    Productive.

    Bat-shit crazy.

    Whatever you want to call waking up with the sun to go jogging on a Saturday morning.

    Sleep was a necessity for me on the weekends. It was like being reborn. After a long week of children screaming about homework and arguing for more points on their last essay, I needed to lose myself in the death of one week and the birth of another.

    It was like my eyes were out of focus, like I was watching myself through someone else. Somehow I had fallen into your routine and abandoned a piece of my own.

JG

Halfway through the jog we stopped for a quick breather at a crosswalk. With both of our heart rates up I came clean, hoping I would survive the embarrassment. "I know I said that I live a few towns over, but I actually live right around the corner."

A truck drove by, spitting black smog into the air as it struggled up the hill. Your laughter was cut short by a car horn as the light changed and one car urged another to make a right on red.

"I know," you chuckled. "I've run past your place. I see your car parked out front all the time."

And then you slid your hand into my shorts and squeezed. We jogged back to my apartment to shower together.

JG

On and off again for two weeks.
> Some mornings you went jogging.
> Some mornings you went showering.
> Some mornings you did both.

JG

Casually, one day, you worked in the fact that you had a boyfriend, made it clear that I was the side dish and he was the entrée.

"Oh," said the fool. "I didn't know."

We hadn't really been dating.

"Of course you didn't know."

Our waitress came over and you ordered a full rack of ribs, dry rub, sweet-potato fries instead of classic.

"And what can I help *you* with?" she asked me.

JG

It turned out he was a friend of mine. Not a good friend, but a friend. When my buddy Chase and his girlfriend Robyn came over to my place for drinks before catching a show in the city they had Andrei in tow.

"Andrei's having some relationship trouble," Chase said, putting his arm around Robyn. "I'm sorry we didn't tell you."

"It's not a problem," I said.

Robyn shuffled on my couch, leaned into Chase. "I think a night out will be good for him. I know I was supposed to bring that friend I was telling you about, and I didn't mean to give your date's ticket away, but you know Andrei's a good guy and he needs this."

"I understand."

This small exchange took place when Andrei left the living room to refill our drinks.

"No, please, sit down. It's the least I can do," he said to me, gathering our four empty glasses and heading for the kitchen.

"So who has he been seeing?" I asked.

"Someone he met at the gym," Chase said.

And that's when Robyn said your name.

JG

On our next date we went to a different restaurant. In the car on the way there I rehearsed different variations of the same sentence in my head. This, I imagine, is something that we all do quite often, rehearse how things might go. Play out the best and worst case scenarios so that we might be a little more ready when we're up to bat and the game is on the line. When I brought up the whole boyfriend thing again you brushed me off, as if I was some child that couldn't get past there being no Tooth Fairy.

Unlike a child, however, I was holding all the cards. Keeping my aces hidden at first—waiting to see what would happen—more curious than spiteful, but definitely not in the mood to be condescended to.

"Not this again," you said. "I've already told you how this is going to be between us. It is what it is and you need to let it go."

"How is Andrei?" I asked.

All of a sudden your eyes got real wide, the shot of panic that comes with any surprise. You wrapped your hand around my wrist and said, "He doesn't need to know."

"How long have you been seeing him?"

"Only a couple of months."

Only.

"Has he told you he loves you yet?"

A hesitation indicated so.

"Have you told him you love him?"

"No. God, no. No way."

I tried to picture myself in his situation. I'm not a hero or a villain—wasn't about to run to Andrei or blow up your spot. He would need to figure it out on his own. You looked at me with expecting eyes, waiting for some cheesy line about how you should be with him instead of me. Waiting for me to say *fuck him* and act like a guy.

Instead, I leaned across the table, freed my wrist, and stood up—stepped aside as much for my sake as for his.

K

KB

I have never dated anyone who wore as much makeup as you. The taste it left in my mouth was unpleasant. Eating product is in no way a turn on. Still, the most frustrating thing was that caking it on robbed your face of all the variables I found so attractive in the first place. With the birthmarks covered and the tiny scar to the left of your nose hidden, I couldn't see the things I enjoyed noticing between kisses the first time we said goodnight.

I left confused, wondering what made you suddenly want to cover up.

L

LW

When you picked me up at a quarter after seven, I had been all but ready to go for a little over an hour. Fourteen different clean shirts lay in a pile on my bedroom floor wondering what they had done wrong as you pulled up.

> You: I'm outside (:
> Me: K be right out

Then I stalled. The last thing I wanted was to appear too eager. Retrieving gum from the pantry, I measured off seconds while chewing.

I spit the gum out.

Opened the door, and walked to your car.

LW

Originally we had planned on going for ice cream. Mike & Jill's parlor was the best place I knew. "They have the most amazing hard ice cream."

"Oh, I don't like hard. I prefer soft."

"Pretty sure they only serve hard stuff there."

We kept driving.

Talking about how you love horror movies and I love rollercoasters. How thrill-seeking can lead you to find unexpected things. Somehow the conversation shifted to *The Lion King*, which we both agreed, was our favorite Disney movie.

"But I hate the part where Scar kills Mufassa."

"Fuck that part," I said.

"What a wonderful phrase."

LW

"There!" I pointed. "Pull in there."

"What's Cups?"

"Just follow me, you'll love this."

As we walked in, the only employee behind the counter eyed us skeptically.

"Can we have some samples?"

She handed me two tiny paper cups, the kind that reminded you of the little bathroom cups with the flowers on them that your mom always used to buy when you were a kid.

What ensued was a sticky, cold mess of flavor on top of flavor. We sampled the frozen yogurt until the paper grew weak and we had to throw the cups away.

LW

"How about the beach?"

      "Anywhere but the beach."

      "Why not the beach?"

      "I just don't like the beach."

      "But I like the beach."

      "Fine, we'll go to the beach."

      "We don't have to go to the beach."

      "We'll go. I want to go to the beach."

      How many conversations went like this?

LW

"If you could pick any one thing to describe me, what would it be?"

"Not answering that," you said.

"Come on, it can be anything. A noun: a person, place, or thing."

There we were in my car. Parked in front of the zoo, with the windows down and the radio off, listening for the animals to call out in the night.

It wasn't a serious question.

"A broken compass," you said.

"A broken compass?"

"Yeah, I think that's pretty fitting. What noun am I?"

"I was thinking maybe like a donkey."

"Oh...well, you're a baboon."

We weren't far off.

LW

We will always have Atlantic City. Before the casinos began closing down for good, we lost our shirts there. Gambled away pieces of the future in exchange for a moment of immortality.

We wrote our initials with our fingers in the wet sand down by the ocean, and when the water washed them away we went back up to the room and wrote our initials on the wall behind the nightstand next to the bed.

LW

That was our thing, not having a game plan. When the wind changed, so did we.

I could never quite figure you out and perhaps that's what drew us together. One minute we would be clicking, going rummage saling—reveling in bargains, pulling discarded treasures out of church basements and singing like thieves as we rode away. The next minute you would be giving it to me for not noticing your new haircut, for failing to put my turn signal on whenever I shifted lanes.

Our friends seemed to envy us. But no one was shocked when I told them we were through.

LW

For Valentine's Day I got you a dozen roses and tickets to see Jim Gaffigan at the New Jersey Performing Arts Center, because you had enjoyed his comedy when we watched his special on Netflix.

The roses were a safe play—that's probably why you never bothered to put them in water. They were wilting on the kitchen table when I came over to pick you up the following weekend for the show.

"You're not dressed?"

"I don't really feel like going."

"Why not?"

I plucked a few heads off the roses, put them in my pocket. You filled the tea kettle, set it on the stove, but didn't turn the gas on. "I just feel a little off tonight."

"And you couldn't have told me sooner? What am I supposed to do?"

"Do whatever you want."

So I called up Chase. I wasn't about to let the tickets go to waste, too.

LW

You read in a magazine that what people fear most in a relationship is running out of things to say.

As if talking is the key to everything.

For me though, it has always been about the writing. When I no longer have anything left to write for the other person, only then, do I begin to worry.

LW

I took no pleasure in breaking your heart. For the last time, I'm sorry. But I had every right to feel the way I felt. What got lost in my task to end things, however, was that you had every right to feel things, too.

LW

It's never easy.

Discarding someone or being discarded. And yet we put ourselves in these situations time and time again.

"Fuck you."

"I had a feeling you'd react this way."

"Oh, just fuck off. Get off your high-horse. This isn't your classroom and I'm not one of your students." You picked up a candle, considered throwing it.

"I wouldn't expect you to understand."

"This is such bullsiht. I never liked you anyway. You're an ass. You're insecure and your laugh makes you sound retarded."

"There's nothing wrong with my laugh."

You threw the candle at the couch. The cushions caught it. "See? Way insecure."

"Oh, I see alright."

What I see is the blind destruction.

LW

From there, it was a race. Game on to see who could find someone else first.

M

MD

The word "enchanted" never meant much to me. I always believed "hypnotized" or "captivated" were much better. They are so much more accurate. What two words can better describe the blinders we wear and the prisoners we are when it comes to the people we care about?

Spring break, freshman year of college, you invited me over your house so I didn't have to spend the money on a plane ticket home. All year long we had been dancing around unspoken feelings. You never knew it but at the end of the fall semester, I picked my classes for spring to be closer to you. Our first night at your house, we sat around a bonfire roasting marshmallows with a group of your high school friends.

Until then you had always been serious. "A bookworm wrapped in a nerd-geek," is how you described yourself when we first met.

But in the comfort of old friends you were playful, full of mischief. You spent the night poking the fire and catching embers as they fell onto your sweater, daring the sparks to ignite. It enchanted me to see you like this. To see a side of you that I had almost missed out on.

MT

You noticed the scar in Panera, a moment after we sat down to coffee.

"And what do we have here?" you asked, tracing the gash the size of an inchworm on the tendons between my knuckles and my wrist. I was ready with my answer, because, while I never notice my scars anymore, other people seem to notice them all the time.

"A hockey skate," I said. "Sliced my hand senior year, when one of my teammates jumped over the bench."

I knew you weren't the one right after I told you. Disappointment flattened your face.

"Oh." You dropped my hand. "I'm not even gonna pretend I know sports."

Perhaps you would have liked it more if the scar had been from a spat with an ex I would rather not talk about. Or maybe, from a piece of loose tile, or a rusty nail, from one of the summers I spent in college contracting bathrooms with my Uncle John.

That's okay, though, because I scored two goals the night I got that scar. And even though I may not notice it so much anymore, I'm glad I have it.

N

NL

They say that whoever develops feelings first is the one who loses.

You were one of the ones who beat me.

NL

No one goes to the train station expecting to meet their first love, and yet, there you were. With your plain jeans and gray t-shirt, your hair cut short and no jewelry on, I could tell that many had overlooked you the same way they had overlooked me.

The old adage goes: *Opposites Attract*, but there really isn't anything scientific about this.

Opposites attract.

Likes attract.

If there's a connection, whoever feels that connection...attracts.

NL

The express to New York, Penn Station.

I'll confess to watching you board the train. To calculating my steps so that I was in the seat across the aisle from you. But it was you who made the first move.

Catching me by surprise with a smile.

Validating the pre-steps I'd taken to put us in a situation where a first move was even possible.

"Where ya headed?" I asked.

"Probably the same place you're headed."

NL

It all started with a kiss at the duck pond.

Sure, we had first met a week earlier, walked around the streets of Manhattan, but that kiss at the duck pond is where the feelings really started.

For me, anyway.

NL

"It was so nice spending the day with you today," you said on the phone. "Driving around your town, walking around the park, seeing how active everything was, it was like a mini-vacation. No one ever does anything in my town."

"I had a lot of fun, too. I really didn't expect anyone else to be up at the park at ten in the morning on a Tuesday."

We lived twenty miles apart in two very different towns. So it took a little effort, but we figured out a way to make things work. The plan was to walk around the park together, talking, enjoying the beautiful day. We were lucky to even find a place to park, because there were old men playing softball on all three baseball fields that the macadam circled.

It was like stumbling upon a secret world. We'd both skipped school hoping to find peace and quiet. Little did we know, things go on in places that we think are quiet while we are away from them. We walked slowly, took in the games one by one and I imagined the old men younger. Each had a story we would never know. First kisses, first loves that would all be forgotten unless someone had taken the time to write it all down. Along the way, the path forked, offered a left turn onto a broken trail that led to an octagon-shaped deck in the middle of a small pond. A fountain shot water into the sky and the sound of water crashing down on water blocked out the sounds of the softball games.

"This is so cool," you said.

"I forgot about this, I haven't been here since I was a kid. It's like a mini-oasis."

Big, swooping willow trees hid us from the park—
we'd found the privacy we were looking for.

"Look, ducks!"

"Yes, ducks." I leaned in.

NL

Just before I kissed you, you whispered, "I've never kissed anyone before."

Five words barely audible over the sounds of the fountain. Whisper sounds on top of slushing sounds, but I was certain I'd heard them.

NL

"There's a scenic overlook on Route 78 close to my house. We can meet there, enjoy the view, figure out what we want to do from there," you suggested.

"Sounds like a good plan."

But even the best plans can be thwarted by the weather. Up until then, it had been sunny. We were lucky.

This time, not so lucky.

Fog ruled the sky. Mist blocked out the view and rendered the overlook useless. It was like staring out an airplane window above the clouds but without the majesty of being thirty-thousand feet off the ground.

There was a nice mall nearby, so we both drove there, parked in front of the Cheesecake Factory, and walked inside.

"Do you want to borrow my hoodie?" I noticed the goosebumps on your arms.

"Would you mind?"

How could I mind? I got to stare at you in my sweatshirt while we walked around the mall, while we ate lunch, while you rested your head on my shoulder and we saw the new Harry Potter movie in the mall's theatre.

And at the end of the day, when you gave my hoodie back, it went home smelling like you.

NL

"You've never had Sarku?" I asked, shocked. "You've been missing out."

"The secret for their business is this guy." I took a free sample from the man passing out small pieces of chicken on toothpicks in the middle of the food court.

Once you tasted it, you were hooked. I bought us two of the Teriyaki special and we sat down and talked about television shows. Friends, we both agreed, was our favorite. You liked Phoebe best because she's different and I liked Chandler best because he's funny. It turned out that we both loved to read and write. Your hooks got a little deeper when you said, "We should write a short story together."

I'd never written anything collaboratively with anyone else before. No one had ever asked me to.

NL

"You've never been in Brookstone?" you said. "Come on, let me take you there. It's like a futuristic store, with all kinds of cool stuff."

We laughed as we sank into anti-gravity bungee chairs.

We wrote little notes to each other on the black-light To-Do-List boards.

We allowed our hands to touch as we built a miniature sand castle out of synthetic sand.

NL

Before we bought the Harry Potter tickets, we walked into the Lego Store. Bright colors lit our faces and the yellow floors hurt our eyes.

"Who makes all of these?" you asked the girl behind the counter, referencing the giant display models in the store.

"Actually, we do," she beamed.

"This must be a pretty fun place to work."

"Actually, it is."

While you told her that you also worked in a mall, at an Auntie Anne's kiosk, I went to the build-your-own Lego people stand. From the thousands of tiny parts, I pieced together a Lego person with your brown hair, your blue jeans, and my red sweatshirt.

"What's this?" you asked, but you didn't wait for me to answer. You went straight to work, piecing me together.

I still have that Lego person. I still have the ticket stub you gave to me after you paid for the movie and said, "Here's something else to remember the day by."

I remember very little of the film.

I was too busy focusing on holding your hand. Still dizzy from when you kissed my cheek and said, "Be mine," just as the final preview was ending and the featured film was beginning.

NL

The first time we slept together was the first time you had slept with anyone. I had never been with someone I cared so much for, and I felt like I had more to lose.

I wonder what's worse, feeling naïve and breakable or being trusted with innocence?

"I don't have much experience," you said, eyes downcast, showing me the top of your head.

"Don't worry about it. You'll figure it out. We just have to get you some confidence."

You tensed, winced as if I had wounded you. "Is it really that obvious? That I'm not a confident person?"

You were adorable and shy, endearing, yet desperate for an answer—as if I'd caught onto something that you worried about quite often.

I never meant to hurt you.

"Whoa, whoa…I was talking about kissing, silly. All you need is a little practice."

I wanted you to see that you were desirable.

There I was shocked that no one had seen what you had to offer. There I was trying to remind myself to slow down the moment, because I was growing more and more certain that you were a dream. At any second I expected my eyes to open—to find nothing but the cruel bleakness of night that greets us after we wake up too soon.

I was amazed at how fast you caught on. "Close your mouth more. Lips on lips. Slow down."

Watching you flounder and then watching you succeed was like planting something and then watching it grow. You blossomed, taking the lead.

You had every reason to be confident.

NL

A week later I wrote: "It all started with a kiss at the duck pond" in a notebook, took a picture of it, and texted it to you.

"Is that the beginning of our story?" you asked.

And that's when I realized that we had been writing our story together all along.

NL

You never thought I could taste the nicotine on your breath. I used to wonder how someone could be with a person who always tasted and smelled like smoke.

You thought you were slick with your gum, but behind the mint I couldn't miss the tangy taste the crave left behind. I enjoyed those kisses so much more than I ever thought I would.

NL

On top of the Mountain Creek ski slopes, there were once two snow angels holding hands.

"Take that!" you yelled, hurling a snowball at me.

Take that!

Take that!

Your voice echoed.

As your words lost their strength, I blitzed, tackling you to the ground where we lay together on our backs, giggling in the snow.

We had taken two cars because we were traveling with a group of your friends and a group of my friends. When it was time to leave, you hugged me goodbye. We had been together for two months, and if you knew it was over at that point, you never let on.

The saddest part is that as I was driving away, my face slowly thawing from the cold, I was so certain I would see you again. There was no need to say goodbye in my eyes.

NL

Breaking up is easy today. All you need to do to break some-one's heart is send a text message. There's no public scene, it's less messy. Yes, it's cold and it's quick and impersonal, but that's exactly the point. There's no clearer way to say, "It's over."

If someone chooses to break up with you through a text message, it really is over.

You couldn't even give me that.

NL

A Yo-yo.

If I had to pick one noun to describe you, that's what it would be. Because after two weeks of not talking or returning any messages, you sent a text saying:

> I'm sorry for disappearing. I'm just going through a lot right now in my life and it's just not my tendency to open up to people, hence the isolation. But when you're going through something, I absolutely don't want you to feel alone the way I feel alone sometimes. So please, talk to me and I promise I'll always be an ear and be there for you.

Except you weren't.

NL

Another week of blackout and I was still reeling, still so confused. I don't know which would have been better. A quick, hard knife stab runs deep but the initial pain is over in a moment, one terrible moment as everything peaks and crashes. A long, slow knife drag hurts less but takes longer to heal. Because you can never be sure exactly when it is over, where the end stops and the healing can begin.

"Hi, Auntie Anne's. Alexa speaking, how may I help you?"

I called your work, asked what time you would be in.

"This afternoon until closing," Alexa said.

I felt a little dirty sleuthing but the cold rush of hope helped me feel good again. After racing through a shower, I got in the car, ready to conquer the twenty miles that stood between us.

Ready to fight for you.

The whole way there I hoped that it would be romantic as hell, like the movies, showing up out of nowhere in the name of love. But when I saw your face, saw how little you wanted to see me, I knew it had been a mistake. A mistake made with the best of intentions.

"Did you need anything in particular?" were the exact words you chose.

"I just wanted to make sure you were alright," I said. "I got these for you."

"You bought me books? You didn't need to get me anything."

Translation: *I don't want to owe you anything.*

You distracted yourself by making pretzels, ran your blade through the soft dough, spun it into the almost heart-like shape of a pretzel.

Alexa listened from a safe distance while she worked. Her hand ready, I'm sure, to call mall security if I upset you too much.

"I'll call you tonight," you said.

But you never did.

NL

After I left the mall, I felt like I had gotten at least part of the closure I was looking for. As I drove further away, however, it became clear that the trip hadn't accomplished either of the two things I had hoped it would. Instead, it left me even more impressed with you than before.

All of our time together, I always felt like the mature one. Like I was showing you how the world worked by teaching you how to kiss.

Dropping in on you at work, seeing you more confident and more comfortable than I'd otherwise seen you, that did it for me. It made you stronger in my eyes. And it became clear that I wasn't going to be able to hold onto you if you felt like leaving.

NL

I thought deleting your number from my phone might help me miss you less.

Eight days later, it came while I was eating lunch.
A text from a number with your area code.
My stomach jumped.

I want to apologize for not calling when I said I would. I'm not good at finding the right words, but you deserve closure and some peace of mind. This is starting to feel like an obligation and that's not what I want this to be. I'm not saying we can't catch up casually, but I can't handle the relationships I already have in my life, let alone new ones. But I still didn't go about things the right way avoiding this altogether for so long.

What you probably meant to say was, "I'm scared."
And what I ached to say was, "Please, don't throw me away."

NL

Finally, after it was clear I'd lost you, I threw away the books I'd bought you, because I got tired of looking at them on my shelf. Before throwing them away, though, I went back and re-read all of the little notes I had written you in the margins throughout. Mini-caricatures and inside jokes. Little things that I pictured you stumbling across while you read late at night, wrapped under a big blanket.

I wonder if that would have changed anything. Had I gotten the books to you sooner, so that you could have seen how much I cared, would that have made you want to stay?

NL

You Tweeted:

> Starting my day off with a little Shel
> Silverstein.

And then posted a picture you'd taken of the poem *Forgotten Language*.

I favorited it. Replied with:

> :)

And then posted a picture I'd taken of the poem *Poet's Tree*.

You favorited it.

And that was that.

My final memory of you is a gold star in a virtual world.

NL

Take that!
> *Take that!*
> Your voice still echoes.

OA

Usually whenever someone would lead with: "What's your sign?" I would take it as a bad sign.

You rebounded fast, however. "Let me start over."

The bartender was looking at us. Eager, I would imagine, to see me shoot you down.

"Are you a library book?" you asked, and right there you had me.

OA

Call it childish and I will take it as a compliment. You went to the checkout line at the grocery store, left me alone in the crowded aisles amongst the old women squinting at coupons and the young boys climbing all over the displays.

When I caught up with you unloading bags from the cart to your car, I was carrying two balloons.

"Where did you get those?"

"Floral Department."

"You're silly," you said. "What're we supposed to do with those?"

"It's a secret. Let's get going."

It was a big night for us. We were to make dinner together at your place. And while I had seen the outside, looked up through the windows whenever I came to pick you up or drop you off, I had yet to come inside.

The fish turned out dry and under seasoned. The meal wouldn't have impressed anyone, but I found beauty in your empty shelves. Gorgeous, deep wooden spaces built into the walls, waiting to house your history in pictures, knick-knacks, and books.

"Oh those," you said. "I told you I just moved in. There's not much to look at yet."

I wiped my sweaty palms on my jeans as I stared at them, flew to dreaming about the fun I might have if I ever had my own spaces like those.

"Are you okay?" You touched my shoulder.

"The balloons! We almost forgot about them."

I untied the string and undid the latex knot, brought the pinched end to my lips and sucked the helium.

You did the same, and we had a serious conversation.

The words came easier like this.

OA

Your entire family—that is: your sister, two brothers, grandfather, grandmother, and mother—all collectively gasped when I sat down at the dinner table and took your father's fork.

"Why don't we find you another fork?" your mother said.

Later, I was told that your father had eaten all of his meals with the same fork for the last twenty years. I was in no position to question it.

"Yeah, that's Dad's fork," your little brother said.

With a dry mouth and a beating heart, I handed your father his fork.

This was strike one.

OA

The more time we spent together, the more I began to feel like I had known you for a long time. My worst days at work were better knowing that you were out there, somewhere, maybe thinking of me.

Seeing you dancing with my little cousins at my aunt's wedding charmed the hell out of me. That night, back at the hotel, I got out of bed as you went to put your shirt back on. There was something in the pocket of my pants—which were puddled on the floor by the nightstand—that I wanted to give you.

"What's this?"

"A key to my apartment," I said.

You took it from me and gave me that *I'm going to have you again* smile.

How was I to know I had made a mistake?

Before we began again, I told you that I thought I loved you. You kissed me and bit my bottom lip as if to punish me for saying it. You fell asleep soon thereafter, leaving me to lie awake as my words hung loose in the air above us.

This was strike two.

OA

Until it happened, I never thought it would happen. It was just something in country songs and B-list crime dramas that always led back to a heartbroken boyfriend being locked away.

Standing there in the doorway, dumbstruck, it wasn't your cheating that bothered me. It wasn't the disappointment that would come with considering the time I'd wasted on you and could never get back.

In that moment the only thing I wanted was the two of you out of my bed. "Get the fuck out! Get out! Get out! Get out! You're out!"

OA

At least he was sorry. Maybe even afraid. He hurried his clothes on while I turned my head, but on his way out we made eye contact. "I had no idea, man. I was told this was a brother's place."

I walked him to the door, you pushed past us both, not saying a word.

"You did me a favor," I told him.

But he was already out and off towards the elevator.

OA

After I put new sheets on the bed, I did a quick inventory of my dresser to make sure nothing had been stolen. Then I took the old sheets to the sink, balled them up, and lit a match.

Fire as therapy—it felt good watching them burn. Once the ashes were down the drain, I saw it on the counter, the key I'd given you. Whether you had forgotten it or left it behind on purpose, I still don't know. The next day I changed the locks anyway.

OA

-Seven years of bad luck.
        -A bloody back of the hand.
        -Fourteen stitches.

        This is what it takes to get over you.

OA

 It took the weekend for me to realize that what you had taken from me wasn't only time. What I really lost that day was security. A scent still lingers like your shampoo. It hangs in the air, mocking me, an ever-present reminder that even when I think things are going so well, I may be wrong.

OA

Chase dragged me out of the apartment by the sleeve of my shirt.

"Get the fuck over it. I know you will, but I'm gonna help you get there faster."

He opened the passenger door to his Toyota, pushed me inside, slammed it shut to drive home his point.

"We're going to the stadium. You're gonna sit your ass in a hard plastic seat and watch the game. I'm gonna feed you beers, and you're gonna forget about everything."

OA

Your hair was everywhere. There were remnants of you in every corner.

P

PM

You played *Hard-to-Get* a little too well. I had been alone for a while when I said, "I want to be with you."

You brushed me off with such coldness, shrugged your shoulders as if you were doing me a favor going out with me. We were complete opposites and still, we were both unhappy. You were used to being pursued and I was used to trying to hold onto things.

So I let go.

I stopped returning your calls, deleted your texts without reading them, went to the movies by myself and laughed along with everyone in the crowd. The result was liberating. I had taken the pressure off, and was surprised to find that things got a little easier.

PM

The *Principle of Least Interest* states: The power in any relationship belongs to the person who cares about the relationship the least.

This is a secret to life.

PM

All of a sudden, you were the desperate one and I was the desirable one.

You showed up unannounced at my door, asking for a second chance, and while I believe in second chances wholeheartedly, my heart had no interest in granting one to you.

When you said, "I'm here now," I had to pinch my leg through my pocket to keep from laughing.

PM

What a relief when you deleted me on Facebook. For weeks I had been wanting to, afraid that doing so would incur your wrath in unforeseen ways. Knowing that you could no longer see my shared personal life was nice. There was also the added satisfaction in knowing that you probably thought you had shown me good by doing this, when actually, some people are just waiting for you to unfriend them.

Q

QS

That's what I called you: "Q."

We weren't made for each other. We weren't soul-mates or hopelessly in love. But we did have a connection.

"What do you want to do for Christmas?" you asked, as the holiday approached. Three weeks wasn't long enough for either of us to spend the special day with the other's family. Three weeks wasn't long enough for either one of us to miss out on Christmas with our own family. Instead, we would both be going to face our relatives alone. Armed with the cryptic phrase: "I'm seeing someone," I told my family about you when they asked what was going on in my life.

"How about we do something Christmas Eve morning," I suggested.

So we met at a diner for breakfast, shared French fries lathered in gravy and sipped burnt coffee.

"I know we agreed not to exchange gifts," you smirked, "but I couldn't resist."

You pulled out an envelope and slid it across the tabletop of the booth. Inside were a dozen bookmarks. I recognized some of them from the racks near the registers at Barnes & Noble. They were glossy, funny, practical.

"Now maybe I won't have to see you using scraps of paper and pieces of napkins in your beloved books."

Smiling, I passed my own present to you across the booth. "I hope ya like 'em, Q."

You opened the Ziploc baggie and found a bunch of pool cue chalk. Together we laughed so loud that the elderly couple sharing an omelet in the booth next to ours asked their waiter if they could pick up their meal and be seated elsewhere.

Bookmarks.

Pool chalk.

Burnt coffee.

I wonder why it can't always be like that. Carefree, like it is in the beginning, when the air feels light and the hope feels drinkable.

That connection allows me to root for you.

QS

Sometimes, though, history can be stronger than a connection. Or at least, it can overpower one.

"I can't make you any promises," you had warned me. "If he wants me back, I'm not sure how I'll feel."

There was no way I could compete with him. Years of history had left me too far behind, even if he only had one foot in the race.

"I'm sorry," you mumbled, as we met for coffee to say goodbye.

"At least you were honest."

That has to count for something.

R

RD

A week before your trip to Italy, your sister's mother-in-law passed away, so you took me instead because the tickets were non-refundable. I wanted to go, not for a free trip, but to see if there could be magic between us. Together, we stormed the old churches—saw Florence, where we should have fallen in love.

I spent the trip making wishes, tossing euros into every ancient fountain, lighting candles along the sides of every altar.

"You're a sucker," you said, as I purchased a shot glass from a curbside vendor. "It's all one big trap."

Did you mean knick-knacks? Relationships? Life? I was never just a tourist along for the ride. It may have looked foolish, but what I was doing was buying up moments I was unsure would ever come again. There were never any traps, only things I walked into willingly.

RD

"You are far too sentimental."

        "Maybe you're not sentimental enough."

        This is what divided us.

RD

The flight home was sobering as we realized there would be no fairytale.

"Thank you," I said, at baggage claim.

"Please, don't thank me."

Our taxis pulled us apart from LaGuardia and we haven't spoken since.

RD

Chase started coming over more and more. Doing his thing, pulling me out of it with simplicity that made me wonder how he had everything so figured out.

"You have to accept the fact that you may never find the right person."

He and Robyn had been together since middle school. Forever, I thought that he was the lucky one. Until, I realized that there are so many dates—memories that mark time—and stories that I will always be able to tell and that he will never have.

RR

If I had anything close to a high school sweetheart, you'd be the one. All of those weekend nights spent kissing in the empty bleachers by the football field amount to that. So much still unknown, and I may get in trouble for saying this, but the most important things we learned in high school didn't happen inside of a classroom. We taught each other so much, but we never quite reached the lessons on love.

Instead, I would have to figure that out on top of a mountain. Playing Battleships on the sofa. Sipping helium out of balloons.

Remember prom? How everyone went crazy trying to figure out special ways to ask who they wanted to go with?

Harris Kristoff asked Portia Aguilar to go with him by leading her on a day-long scavenger hunt during school. He left clues that took her into the boy's locker room, to the vice principal's office, out beneath those same bleachers. It all led back to homeroom, where they sat next to each other. You and I shared that class with the two of them. After she said "Yes," Portia passed the last clue Harris had given her around so everyone could read it:

```
Room 2313.
Sometimes what you've been looking for has
been right there all along.
```

Some asked their dates bluntly, "Do you want to go to prom with me?"

Some did it with flowers or in car window soap. I even saw one girl Post-it note her boyfriend's locker.

Prom?	Prom?	Prom?
Prom?	Prom?	Prom?
Prom?	Prom?	Prom?
Prom?	Prom?	Prom?
Prom?	Prom?	Prom?

Of course, not everyone said yes.

We all didn't find the answers we were looking for.

There was something profound in the way it went for us. How all I said was, "Pick you up at seven."

And you nodded, "Yep."

I never even had to ask.

RR

Together, we weren't the most handsome couple. Whether that is to blame on my lankiness or your cute lack of height is still up for debate. People did their share of staring that night, but we didn't let that keep us from going to prom and we didn't let it keep us from dancing. Together, we lost ourselves for a few hours.

That was our way of saying, "Fuck you, too."

And I'll tell you what, the memory of that "Fuck you, too" lasted much longer than any hate aimed in our direction.

RR

"When do you want to leave?" I asked.

A half hour after prom started, kids began bleeding out the front door in twos and fours, headed for shore houses.

"What time did Marquel tell us to get down there?" you asked.

That's right, we weren't martyrs. We may not have been the most handsome couple and looks may have come our way, but we still had plans. Friends. A place to go.

"He said he'd aim to get there around eleven, so any time after that because the house is in his name."

"Let's stay a while then, we've got all night. No one's going to sleep tonight."

Prom ran from 8:00-10:00.

By 10:08 we were on the parkway driving fast, sipping Red Bulls.

Grabbing that second wind.

Determined to make one night live forever.

RR

We both had a poor sense of direction. By 10:45, I admitted, "We're lost."

"That's just fine," you said.

Minutes before midnight, we pulled into the crowded gravel driveway that crunched beneath my old Pontiac's tires, relieved not to have been the last ones to arrive.

"The pact," Marquel had said, "is that no one starts drinking until everyone gets down there."

"I'm just glad it wasn't us," I mumbled as we carried our bags up to our room.

"This is going to be epic."

RR

You were right when you said, "No one's going to sleep" that night, but most of us did make use of the beds.

When you and I emerged, fifteen minutes later, everyone was drinking. As I poured us both a shot of something fruity, you stopped me, held me by the shoulders, and got all serious. "I think…I'm pregnant," you said.

We both broke out laughing.

"How long have you been waiting to use that line?" I asked.

"About a month."

"Cheers," I said. "To the baby."

RR

"I understand."

"I'm sorry," you said.

"No, don't be. It's understandable."

What we were trying to say was, *We both knew that this probably wouldn't last forever.*

"I've always dreamed of going away to school and they gave me a full academic scholarship. I can't pass this up."

"I wouldn't want you to pass it up for me."

Unless you want to pass it up for me.

But you didn't.

We held onto each other through the shortest summer of our lives. Pretended like the middle of August was further away than it really was—like it would never come.

Until it did.

And you boarded the plane.

Took off without looking back.

RR

Seven days before you left, we took a ride up to Stokes State Forest and walked the trails. Neither of us had enough foresight to bring a hat or a change of clothes, and the sun beat down on us hard that day whenever it could find its way through the tree leaves. The humidity didn't help, and by noon we had soaked through our shirts.

So we took them off and laid them out on these big fat boulders so that they would dry fast while we ate a picnic lunch. Even now, I can remember the way the dirt stuck to your leg. The way things felt in the woods like they had beneath the bleachers, like there were eyes all around us but we somehow remained invisible. What sticks with me most, though, is how many times you checked to see if the shirts were dry.

Four?

Five?

Six times?

That was my first taste of heartbreak.

You could hardly wait to put your shirt back on. It was a subtle indication that I had already lost the right to touch you.

By the time we finished eating, they had dried enough to wear again. It's crazy how meaningful things slip away with the pull of a shirt. You turned away, gave me your back as you tugged it over your head, and that was my last privileged look at you.

You took something out of your pocket and started making your way down the trail.

"What have you got there?" I huffed, catching up.

You were facing a tree, seemed to be punching or clawing at it with whatever you were holding.

"R." I read on the tree.

You kept carving.

Another "R."

Soon both sets of our initials punctuated the primitive paper that was the bark, and for a brief moment I thought that everything was going to be okay. Whether that tree has since fallen or stands to outlive us both, I will never know. But what I do know is that forgetting you was a lot like falling for you. It happened gradually.

RR

Now, it's been years since I've seen you. The other day, online, I saw pictures of your daughter. She has your nose, your strong cheekbones, and someone else's eyes. That brought me back to you, had me plucking my high school yearbook off the shelf reserved for my most important books.

We never even signed one another's, because that would have been too difficult.

There was a picture of us holding hands at a pep rally, after the photos of the athletic teams. I had dog-eared the corner of the page, and the book fell open to it. There we were, together after all this time. Is there anything we wouldn't give to be that young again?

S

SB

The snow was a monkey wrench. A curveball when we had been expecting a fastball. Instead of walking the streets, we settled for the crowded halls of the mall a week before Christmas.

I found you in the back of J-Crew, where you said you would be, holding a winter jacket that looked much too small. You had taken other items to the back of the store with you, laid them out on a display of t-shirts where they did not belong. Long sleeve checkered shirts, leather gloves, those fuzzy slippers which my feet always seemed to yearn for but I never had the guts to spend fifty-dollars on.

Without care, you tossed the jacket aside, added it to the pile of refugee items, and led me out of the store. I kept my eyes down at your heels, feeling sorry for whoever it was that had to clean up your mess.

SB

As I walked you to your car—after we had grown tired of the mall halls—I readied myself for what would come next. I wanted to get closer to you and had no idea why. There were no hints in your body language that you wanted me to kiss you. So I stood there waiting, until you opened your arms and hugged me goodbye.

I drove home with the radio off, drunk on the disappointment of a missed opportunity.

SN

Science was never my best subject. When we were together, I always felt like one giant experiment, someone you were playing with while you passed the time waiting for someone better to come along. You wanted to see if you could make me care about you. See how fast you could make me love you by saying the right thing at the perfect moment.

Like when I said that kissing someone in the rain was one of my biggest fantasies. Later that night, I caught you with my laptop in your lap.

"What're you doing?" I asked.

"Nothing," you said. "Go back to sleep."

But when I wouldn't, you handed me the computer and acted as if I'd committed some grand crime by spoiling the surprise.

"Weather reports?"

"I was trying to figure out where it was supposed to rain around here, tomorrow."

Well done.

Little things like that meant the world to me, and you knew it. If I was just a game to you, you played me well.

SN

After you were sure that I had developed real enough feelings for you, you carried out phase two of the experiment by not answering my calls.

Even worse, you stopped answering my texts. Without warning, the little messages back and forth that had become such a relied upon part of my day were taken away. The saddest part was that I blamed myself, wondered what it was that I had done wrong. When really, you were just measuring my reaction, seeing how many unanswered texts I would send, how many unanswered voicemails I would leave before getting the hint.

SN

Contact.

A place where two points meet.

Still, there is something so cold and distant about this single word. As if it is housed all by itself inside of an empty room.

SN

There is always a specific moment—after things have ended—that I can point to and say, *That's it. That's where one of us made a mistake and something changed.*

At your best friend's New Year's Eve party you spent the last moments of the dying year making fun of me, telling embarrassing stories that I felt you had not yet earned the right to tell.

"…and then his mom says that when he was nine-years-old she walked in on him trying on her makeup!"

"Get out! Did she really?"

"Uh-huh, next thing I know she gets up from the dinner table, leaves us all sitting there eating, and comes back two-minutes later waving a photograph. 'He never even saw me standing there in the doorway,' she says. So she was able to snap a picture and boy you should of seen the look on his face!"

Smiling along, I wondered if this is what it would be like with you every time we went out to have a good time with other people. We do that all the time, test each other to see just how much we can get away with. Was I the kind of guy who would stand to look bad so that you could look good? Could I be walked on if your footsteps were hidden behind a smile or a laugh? These were questions you wanted answers to, and it went beyond me not being able to laugh at myself.

Around eleven-thirty your mood swung in my favor. Dropping a heavy arm over my shoulder, you told me, "At mim-midnight I'm going to kiss you."

When the ball dropped, you did, and I brought in the New Year comforted by the idea of kissing someone else.

I tried my best to learn from my mistakes, to leave little markers along the sides of the road with the hope of not making the same wrong turn more than once. But wrong turns are inescapable when you are lost and looking for something as essential to life as love.

SN

"I was just joking, you know. Trying to be funny."

"Well, har, har, har."

"You need to lighten up."

"You had no right."

"Seriously, you need to lighten up."

"Seriously, why don't you have another drink?"

"Sometimes you're such a little drama queen."

"Ouch."

"See."

What I didn't see at first was that the blind destruction has eyes. It takes aim and looks to do as much harm as possible.

SN

I slammed the door to your apartment and walked out.

"Where do you think you're going?"

You chased me to the elevator, but I had nothing to say to you. When the door opened, you followed me in, pressed every button so that it would be a long, slow ride down. I got out at the next floor and headed for the stairs.

"Stop being such a baby! You're not going anywhere!"

"I have an eye doctor's appointment," I said.

"Bullshit!"

Bullshit. The stairwell echoed.

"You're a loser and you're not going anywhere!"

It was nine stories and I knew that you were too indolent to chase me. Soon, all I could hear were the punctuated last words of your sentences.

SN

Every relationship deserves its grieving period.

There were some that I struggled with, that consumed me for some time once they were over. That's all part of a broken heart. There's no shame in telling someone that they were hard to get over.

But it was different with you. Instead of breaking my heart, you sliced it. Took the narrow sliver of an arrow just missing its intended target.

Once I assessed the damage, realized that I only felt hit—wasn't actually hit—you were buried and grieved for in the time it took me to press:

-phone
-contacts
-S
-edit
-delete contact

SN

There were frustrations.

        There was fucking.

        But most of the time it was just fucking frustrating.

T

TJ

Michelle had known you since grade school, back when you were eight-year-olds running around playing kickball at recess. She had known me since our first semester of college, when we were both freshmen stumbling through eighteenth century novels like *Pamela* and *Robinson Crusoe*.

When I went over her house for dinner that night, I had no idea what she had planned, and judging from your reaction, neither did you.

"I'd like you to meet someone," she said to each of us—to both of us.

"I knew you were up to something," you said to her. "You're usually much more chatty during the day when we shop."

It took a moment for me to understand what was going on. Despite everything, I believe in love at first sight, but that was not how it went for us. It was a setup in every sense of the word, and it felt like she'd pointed a loaded gun at my head.

"I've been wanting to introduce the two of you for some time now."

So that's where Michelle had been all morning. Before meeting me for lunch she had been shopping with you. She had been out with both of us the same day, prepping us in the special way we each needed to be prepped. She must have felt confident about us—outlined enough of our edges to know that we would be a good fit.

Because she was as smooth as a baby boy's face when she asked me, "What're you doing tonight?"

"Nothing yet."

"Why don't you come over my place for dinner? I'm making tacos."

I wonder how often that happens. How often is the person sitting right across the table from you up to no good?

TJ

"Names," Michelle said.

We had forgotten that formality. Both of us were probably plotting ways to get back at her.

Or ways to give back to her.

What single friends do I have?

Sometimes having the loaded gun of a setup pointed at us is exactly what we need.

TJ

I don't know why she chose tacos. Of all the meals she could have prepared, why had she chosen the sloppiest of things to eat?

On the surface it seemed like an oversight, something so silly to have not considered if she was going through all that trouble hoping that there would be sparks between us.

Or maybe that was exactly the point.

To disarm us from the beginning.

Nothing either of us could say in a first conversation could have been any more embarrassing than the sights and sounds of a taco dinner.

"Napkins!" she said, leaving the room. "We need more napkins."

When we were alone, you blushed. Cheeks turning the color of the pink wine she had poured in our glasses.

From there, things blossomed.

TJ

One morning, we decided to wake up early and meet in a corner of the public library. The rain outside gave the whole place that musky wet paper smell that always gets me high. You found me in the back left corner surrounded by the words of a thousand dead poets.

"Fuck. My sketchbooks."

The water had claimed them. You slid down with your back against a shelf, joined me on the floor, and we mourned together.

"These are really good," I said.

"Maybe they were."

"I think it's cool, the way they're smearing. Like they're all part of a series. It ties them together."

You considered this. I pulled an unlined notebook out of my backpack and handed it to you. "Draw me something. Don't worry, we'll run it under some water later so it fits in with the rest of them."

I angled myself toward you so that you couldn't see what I was writing, laid my own notebook across my knees, and wrote:

This may work.

TJ

That first summer, I said, "I've never seen the water this blue."

You smiled as you looked up from your paperback novel, then put your head back down and continued on reading. Not every address requires a response. We had reached that stage.

"I mean, the Jersey shore is supposed to be green, or at least a darker color. It's definitely more blue."

"Maybe it's your sunglasses," you joked. "Take them off and tell me what you see."

Instead, I turned my attention toward the seagulls playing tag down by the waves. We both knew why the water looked bluer. We were going to let the moment pass but suddenly I wanted something to let me know you felt the same way, too. Reassurance that I hadn't made the whole thing up.

Without missing a beat, you said, "Definitely bluer" and turned the page.

TJ

"If you could change one thing about me, what would it be?"

"That's a loaded question," I said.

Relationships are full of them. Land mines where if you answer you're screwed no matter what you say.

"Come on. I promise I won't get mad."

"Oh, I'm not falling for that."

"Alright, if you could change one thing about yourself, what would it be?"

Now that was a question I could answer. But telling you what I would change about myself would make me vulnerable. Our relationship was still in its infancy, we were so caught up in everything we liked about each other. It seemed silly to start taking risks while things were going so well.

Not answering, though, would have been risky also. Because trying to preserve the present can often damage the future.

This was your way of saying, *I'm ready to take this to the next level—past all the things we like about each other.*

I sighed.

Aimed my eyes at the ceiling.

"If I could change one thing about myself it would be…"

I took the risk.

TJ

It didn't take long. Soon Michelle faded into the background of *Us*, and now when I think of you and me, I no longer think of her.

She had to have known there was a chance that might happen if those sparks ignited. The most selfless thing a friend can do is give one person to another, knowing that they themself might lose something because of it.

TJ

"If I could change one thing about myself it would be…"

I lowered my eyes from the ceiling, thirsty to measure your reaction as the words left my lips for your ears.

"…how inadequate I feel with the game on the line. I always seem to find the right words after a moment has passed. I don't know what it is but sometimes I freeze up. Like I'm saying what I think I want to say and a few minutes later, after it's too late, I think of something better. Something that would have fit my feelings a little more accurately and maybe made a difference communicating something important."

Your forehead crinkled the way it does when you're unsure of something. I sat there feeling as if I had been tricked, embarrassed. Until your brow flattened and you said, "Try waiting ten seconds longer."

"What do you mean?"

"Just take a little longer before you take that swing with the game on the line, it might make a difference. Or it might not. Who knows?"

I try to apply this advice whenever I can. Sometimes it works but more often than not it doesn't matter. Ten seconds just isn't enough time. A few minutes *is* enough time. But we don't always have a few minutes, and that's just something I'll have to live with.

TJ

Lost in literature, I believe, is what you called me.

"Your head is always so buried in a book or notebook that half the time when I leave you I worry that you'll walk face first into traffic and I'll never see you again."

All serious, you threw your hands up in the air and said, "Unbelievable" as I started giggling.

That was it for me.

Right there in that moment I was sure that I loved you.

There had, of course, been prior moments when I felt love for you, where my heart had given all the appropriate signs that it was vulnerable—falling. But right then, with your arms flailing, clapping grumpily against your thighs as they came back to your sides, I was more certain than I'd ever been before. Not because you cared about me, but because it was clear that you got me. You understand who I am, and there is nothing quite as gratifying as this.

TJ

Before long, I grew to love the Question Game. It was mind-boggling how much I would learn about you and how much some of my own answers surprised me about myself.

"Flight or invisibility?" I asked.

My personal choice would have been invisibility. A chance to come and go unnoticed whenever I pleased. Secretly, though, I hoped you would choose flight.

I imagined you carrying me, wrapping your arms around me as I held my arms out as wide as they could go.

"Flight," you answered, and my heart soared.

TJ

We don't only talk about super powers, though, and it isn't always fun.

"If you had to pick between losing your eyesight or losing your hearing, what would it be?"

This question upset me. I thought of changing the subject and mumbled, "I don't want to play this game anymore."

But you never let me off the hook. You were hard on me with: "You have to answer."

The thought of a world without music saddened me but the thought of a world without light terrified me.

"Hearing. Definitely rather lose hearing."

That question stuck in my head the next few days, as if it were waiting for me to change my mind. I struggled with it on my way to work, in the shower, before bed when my eyes closed and my mind was still open.

Depth.

Challenge.

Unexpected things of tremendous value. For a little while I saw things more clearly. From time to time, I still do.

TJ

One thing I never told you was just how low I was when you found me. Just before you, I had spent a long time feeling alone, meeting and going on dates with all of the wrong people. Accumulating bitterness and dropping off jagged little pieces of hope along the way.

"I'm thinking of giving up," I confided to Michelle.

She gritted her face, pouted her mouth in an angry half-frown.

"Maybe I'm just not meant to find what I'm looking for."

That's when she first mentioned you. Not by name, not by initial, but before you, there was the notion of you. "I'm going to fix you up with someone."

My whole life I had been dreaming, had felt pulled toward something. Holding on to that fragile hope that patience would somehow pay off.

Your face was blurry and your name changed with the wallpaper of every room, but we go back a long time, you and I. The dreamer in me likes to think that we would have found each other without Michelle's help. But if our paths had never crossed, I'd in all likelihood still be out there wandering.

Wondering where the hell you are.

TJ

When you said it back, it was like you had released whatever ropes and chains had been holding up a drawbridge. It shouldn't be possible for such little words to carry such weight, to stand for so much, yet they somehow do. Throughout my life they had come hard, had come easily, come prematurely, come unwanted, and come unrequited. But before, they had never come so forcefully—so eager for expression that the words still hang jittery in my shoulders when I see you until I give the feeling voice.

"I love you."

"I love you."

I love you.

I love you.

I love you.

I love loving you.

I love saying I love you.

You. You. You.

Like a drug, I love you.

I never want to stop saying I love you.

Because I love you.

"I love you, too."

TJ

There was a period of about two weeks before it happened where we both saw it coming. Neither one of us, however, had initially been willing to suggest that next step.

It had to be you.

I had been in relationships where I had pushed too far too fast, where I had been way ahead of the other person and failed to slow myself down. Tempering my excitement over you was difficult, but in the long run it was worth it. Eventually, you caught up—we got back on the same page.

Finally, when you were confident enough that I would say yes, you were direct with: "We should move in together."

And I was ready with that week's apartment listings circled in red.

TJ

There is no need to press your political opinions onto me. You are not going to convince me that all guns are bad, or that Obama has done even a not-so-bad job running the country.

The same thing goes for your counterparts and everything they stand for. If you ask me, each party needs to take a step toward the center, bend a little because the willingness to be flexible is everything.

It may not be the best way to handle things—to ignore the world's problems—but each person has their own way of getting through the day.

This is why I bury my head in a book or notebook, not just because it makes me feel good, but because it allows me to escape, if only for a little while.

TJ

"Violà!" you shouted from the other room. "'Tis complete."

"What are you going on about in there?"

"Why don't you take a break from your precious hockey game, come in here for two minutes, find out for yourself?"

"It's a hockey-*documentary*," I corrected, reaching for the remote. "Give an inch and they take a mile!"

"Oh hush. Get yer cute ass in here."

"Is that a request or an order?"

It really was quite impressive.

"All fifty-two cards." You folded your arms across your chest.

I tossed the almost-empty card-box toward you. "Hey, Brunelleschi, you forgot the jokers."

Arms uncrossed. Refolded again.

"Joker's don't count."

"They're cards aren't they?" I teased.

"*You're* a joker…and also an *ass*."

"Burn."

"Ughhh."

"Really though, it's extraordinary."

We counted ourselves among the lucky. The ones who had either called out sick or been called by work and told to stay home. A snowstorm had quieted the city, rocked it to the brink of sleep before the husky plows and fraught public buses rescued its reputation.

From our apartment we took bets on the children warring in the park below, cheered for our sides, mourned our losses when the snowballs stopped flying, even though our voices could not be heard.

The time we normally spent at work—on other people—we spent on ourselves, me on the couch reading Khaled Hosseini and you at the table with a thousand-piece jigsaw puzzle as the foundation for your house of cards.

Then, without warning, you flicked a corner with your finger before I could snap a picture. Numbers, Jacks, Kings, Queens, shattered in slow motion. Pulling up the puzzle-floor from the table, the pieces crumbled through your fingers like sand back into the box.

"What an incredible waste of time." I couldn't help myself.

"*Hockey* is an incredible waste of time."

"You. Take. That. Back." Deliberate steps in your direction.

"Touch me and I'll scream bloody murder."

Idle threat, I drew closer still.

We wasted what was left of the day on each other.

TJ

Your stubbornness.

If I had to change one thing about you it would be this.

Apologizing first is not as difficult as you make it out to be. You wouldn't be giving anything paramount away by allowing me a small victory. You have no problem saying "I'm sorry, too" but it wouldn't kill you to just say "I'm sorry."

TJ

If I am lost in literature then you are my greatest reason to leave the pages and return to the real world.

TJ

"Turn the fucking light off."

You rarely raise your voice to me, but when you do it has an impact.

I stepped out of the bathroom while I waited for the shower to warm. I must have looked ridiculous, but something in my eyes must have said, *You don't understand,* because the look in your own eyes softened from *I'm going to kill you* to *I can't believe we're about to have another fight about this.*

"I just don't see why you have to leave the lights on in rooms you're walking out of. The living room, the bedroom, the kitchen."

"Honestly?"

"Yes, honestly." You wanted an answer.

"I'm afraid of the dark."

Your forehead crinkled. "Oh."

I closed the bathroom door and by the time I got out of the shower you were tucked in bed watching reruns of *The Big Bang Theory*. When I stepped into the hallway I had to squint to find our bedroom.

You had turned on every light in the apartment.

TJ

When I was little, I used to do it whenever I was nervous. Scratch sporadically at the inside of my arm where my elbow bends. My mother would point it out to me, try to keep me from hurting myself. "Honey, you're doing it again."

It happened most often on Sunday nights before a new week of school began, or out on the baseball field whenever there were runners on base and I was expecting the ball to be hit to me.

It is a habit I must have never fully outgrown. Because there are times when you get nervous before a big day at work or a family function, and I catch you reaching for the inside of your arm.

That's when it hits me. I am as much a part of you as you are of me.

TJ

There were times when I doubted us. Where I didn't know if we would make it.

Moments when I would catch myself wondering if this was what I had fought so hard for, if I would always have to keep fighting for it.

There were times when someone at a dinner party would catch my ear by reciting a line from Keats or Yeats, and I would want to get to know that new person better.

And then there were the times I would walk into my classroom to find one of my colleagues walking out, and I knew you had put them up to something. I would flick on the lights and there would be an *I LOVE YOU* written on the whiteboard, with a reminder for me to call you later, and a footnote telling me what to pick up for dinner on my way home from work.

All those times when I would find our initials written in the steam on the bathroom mirror, circled by a poorly drawn heart.

Tell me, did you ever have any doubts?

TJ

The lights on.

 The lights off.

 Eyes open.

 Eyes closed.

 For some, these things matter. Like the way you always have to have music on.

 "Change the song. I hate this song," you say.

 "What song?"

 When my hands are in your hair and my skin is against your skin, I no longer feel like the needy one.

TJ

Just once, I broke the rules and asked you the same question. Normally, we weren't allowed to do this, steal one another's moves when we played the game. It took away from the sport of it, coming up with new things to ask. But you made an exception and answered anyway.

"Your mouth," you said.

"My mouth?"

"Yes. If I could change one thing about you, I would change this."

I didn't understand. Relishing the moment, you let me hang there, lingering in the gray area between self-defense and self-doubt.

"Sometimes, when you get excited, it just happens. I get that. You can swear if you smash your hand with a hammer or lose your keys, and I even encourage your dirty mouth in bed. But cursing at the TV every minute of a hockey or football game is something I'm prepared to leave you over."

TJ

You have yet to offer up what it is you would most like to change about yourself.

That's okay for now, but maybe one day soon, I will ask.

TJ

"B-9," you called out.

"Miss. I-7."

"Miss. C-8."

"Missed again. H-7."

"Miss. D-7."

"Another miss," I said.

"You're moving the ships again."

"That's absurd. J-7."

"I told you the secret is to always shoot in angles. You don't stand a chance otherwise."

"Miss or hit?"

"You're moving the ships again, I know it. Let me see your board."

"No way. Is it a hit or a miss?" You still hadn't said.

"You're eventually gonna run out of places to switch that 5-ship to."

"You just stay on your side of the couch," I threatened.

You missed four more times.

Eventually, you hit.

TJ

"What is this?" you asked, pulling a box out from beneath our bed.

"Oh, that...that's nothing."

"Doesn't look like nothing."

You removed the lid and pulled out a picture of two people holding hands.

"This is great. Did you photograph this?"

"No," I said.

You removed several other items from the box: a few dried roses, a few movie ticket stubs, a Lego man, a teddy bear with a bracelet around its neck.

"Oh, I get it."

I didn't know what to say.

"Am I in here?" you asked.

"Of course not."

Without another word you put the top back on, slid the box back under the bed. Let my past rest in the past.

TJ

There was no explanation as to why your office out of the blue decided that all door-stops were fire hazards.

This seemed unjust.

So I slipped into your office the next day—quite easily because the secretaries that guarded the entrance had a thing for me at the Christmas party—to pass out doorstoppers to everyone on your floor.

"Have you gone mad?" You were cute all red, fiery. "Great. My boss is gonna fire me."

I shushed you, gave you my most roguish grin. "They aren't doorstoppers, they're paperweights."

Together we showed them.

TJ

It is what we are doing when we order Chinese food and sit cross-legged on the floor in the living room by the coffee table with the shades drawn to block out the moon, the lights off, and candles lit. We're doing it when you say, "I'm bored," and I suggest we go for a drive without any place to go and we end up with a flat tire a half-mile from the nearest motel and you say, "Carry me, since this was your brilliant idea." Or quite literally it is what we are doing when you buy the do-it-yourself furniture made out of compressed particle board from Ikea and we have to put the pieces together ourselves. Only then, we are building shelves, and the building of shelves, too, becomes a part of our history.

TJ

Is it paper or clocks? Not even Hallmark could give me a straight answer.

"Well sir, traditionally the one-year is paper but more recently—more modernly, sir—people have been moving toward clocks."

"Clocks?"

"Yes, sir," the associate told me over the phone. "The gift of time or something."

"Paper or clocks…" I mumbled.

"You still there, sir?"

Stupidly—hopefully—I continued. "And how about the second?"

"The two-year is cotton traditionally…or china."

I thanked her and hung up the phone, thought of so many things I could do with cotton balls, tried to stop myself from thinking that far ahead. Not that I believe in jinxes, but there was no need to risk it.

At Macy's I picked out an alarm clock for myself that was "Guaranteed to wake you and not your partner."

Without much confidence, I charged it to my credit card, hoping that I would no longer startle you out of sleep every morning with the alarm on my iPhone, and went home to think about paper.

Origami? I could figure out how to fold flowers or construct those little cranes.

Words on paper? No. I gave those to you nearly every week in one form or another.

Finally, I decided to give you a stack of quality stock paper, hole-punched, spiral bound, with a different year written at the top of every page.

"What happens after year eighty?" you asked.

The pages stopped there.

Rolling my eyes, I said, "Really?"

You kissed me and said, "I love it. I made this for you, too."

Beside you was a pillow that I had not noticed until you placed it in my lap. "Have at it," you said, handing me a pair of scissors.

And when I gave you a confused look you motioned with your fingers: "Cut it open."

I still don't know exactly how you did it. The apartment had been empty when I called Hallmark, yet somehow you'd read my mind and knew to fill the pillow with cotton balls.

Breathless, I looked up, eyes blurring as you hid a big grin behind a coffee mug.

"And I also got you a watch."

TJ

Part of me will always wish for you to be the one who messes this up. If experience has taught me anything it's that it is only a matter of time before one of us blows it.

Often, I remind you of this.

"Shut up," you say. "Neither one of us is going to mess this up. You only need to get this thing right once."

U

There aren't many people with names that start with "U," but there are so many *Yous* along the way.

U

Here's to all of those times when I didn't feel like kissing you or being kissed by you, but I let you kiss me anyway.

V

VC

Many think that a movie is a bad place for a first date because it eliminates all chance of conversation. Even so, we risked all we had because we had nothing to risk. We had come from our separate ways just to see what would happen, and if nothing happened we knew we would be leaving the same way we came. At the end of the night when I asked if there would be a second date, you told me that you didn't think there would be.

"I just didn't feel a connection," you said.

And I understood.

VF

One rule I always tried to keep was: *Keep work separate*. But at an end-of-the-year faculty party, I lost track of this. I had seen you around before, at workshops that brought teachers from the high school and teachers from the middle schools together.

There was never a ring on your finger.

On the strength of a few Long Island iced teas, I started a conversation with you about students who may look promising next year.

"What are your plans for the summer?" I asked.

"Probably going to catch up on some reading. More free time and all. Maybe going to California for a few weeks to visit my boyfriend's family."

Of course, you were already seeing someone.

W

WK

Seventh grade.

By my locker on the third floor after history class. Earlier in the day, I had spotted you at your locker trying to force your winter coat into the tight metal cubby.

"You can put that in my locker, if you want," I said.

"Are you sure that's okay?"

"Yes. It's okay."

"I think we have history together."

"We do have that together."

"I can pick it up right after that then, before last period. So you don't have to wait around after school."

"Here." I took your arm, scribbled three numbers on it. "Just in case I'm not there to open it."

But I was, and there we were.

"Thanks," you said, as I handed the jacket back to you.

That's when you kissed me. It caught me off guard.

My first kiss.

"Thanks," I said.

You dashed down the stairs and I ended up with detention for being late to my last class.

WM

A relationship initially begins by learning a person's story. There were the things you told me, like your favorite bands and movies. And there were the things I learned about you myself, like that you were forced to grow up much sooner than you should have.

After I began coming around, I would help your brother with his English homework when he got home from school. And, because you were never any good at sports, it was me who taught him how to throw and hit a baseball before dark.

It was a two-way street you never knew about.

As we played catch, he would tell me all of your secrets, cue me in on the embarrassing stories that I could ask about later when you and I were alone. He was my informant and I was his friend. He told me his secrets, too.

WM

When you were little, your mother used to change all of the decorations in the house in accordance with the next holiday season. One day you would go to school, return home, and *BOOM!* all Halloween all at once. Unless it was December, or February, or whatever month Easter makes a habit of falling in. You could never trust Tuesdays, because her day off from work was always a Tuesday.

She did it because your grandmother was a cold woman, and she was hoping to fill your childhood with the memories she never had growing up.

Perhaps this is a reason to have children, who wouldn't want the chance to build the perfect childhood?

She told me this when you stepped away to use the bathroom and I couldn't help loving her. Returning a moment later you found us, old friends cracking jokes over coffee.

"What's so funny?" You wanted to know.

What was funny was that I wasn't just falling in love with you—I was falling in love with your family, as well.

WM

There was never a time when I wanted to hear about your ex-boyfriends. While it seems to be part of the schema for getting to know someone new, I am of the minority that would rather pretend they do not exist.

WM

Quickly, we found out that you needed to cuddle and I needed my space. So I would hold you close as we slept all those nights after sleeping together. Only, I could not sleep. Unable to get enough air, no matter how hard I breathed, I suffocated in silence so as not to wake you.

This inherent difference between us both traces back to our parents. My family was close—too close. In my house growing up, everyone was so involved in everyone else's business. There was no mental privacy. Because of this, I am a firm believer that such a thing called *too-much-closeness* exists.

Your father, on the other hand, had run off when you were four. You told me: "My first memory is of him leaving. Not of him actually walking out the door, but of my mom realizing what had happened and saying, 'Shit.' When I asked her what was wrong she threw a piece of paper in the trash and said, 'Dad's left,' and then I said, 'Shit.'"

"I would rather have had too-much-closeness than a broken family," you said.

While I agreed to a certain extent, I feel the need to tell you that all families—I think—are at least a little bit broken.

And the jagged pieces that cut us leave their scars behind.

WM

It was my fault for answering your phone. You were in the shower, I heard it ring.

The number on the screen read: *Unknown*, yet I knew who it was when I answered.

"You're the new ass, I'm guessing."

"That would be me, I guess."

"Good for you, buddy. Tell the heartbreaker to go to hell."

"Will do. There is no need to growl."

"Whatever, buddy. Enjoy the sloppy seconds."

"Will do, again. You take ca—"

He hung up.

You shut the water off as I searched for him by name. I was going to block his number on your phone even though that wasn't my call.

But I couldn't find him.

You had already deleted him as a contact.

WM

The wine had come and we needed a toast. Off the top of your head you said something meaningful, impressive. Attractive.

"Here's to all of the hatchets that seem to never stay buried."

Is it possible that these words just came to you? Or did you have them queued up?

WM

"We may be in trouble," you said, and I knew we were.

"Maybe we can get past this. Push through."

Your mouth tightened as you tried to force a smile. I shook my head and said, "I can't believe this is going to end."

"But it doesn't have to. At least not entirely."

"I just don't understand why we can't get to that next level."

"You can't force it. I love you, but I am not in love with you."

"I know," I said.

So we agreed to stay friends, because we both knew that the love we had for one another was real, even if that was as far as we could take it.

Over time, what started out as a cheap consolation prize, turned into something just as meaningful.

WM

Disappointment.
> Longing.
> Denial.
> Closure.
> Excitement.
> Moving on.

We could give one another a thousand anecdotes for each.

In the middle of the night—after I finally fell asleep—you would roll over and kick me. Eyes shut tight, I would pretend to still be dreaming. As if you hadn't woken me, even though we both knew you had.

WM

I promised myself I wouldn't miss you.
  I promised myself I wouldn't let myself get attached.
  I promised myself I knew what I was doing.
  These were always the hardest promises to keep.

WM

You held me as my brother passed away. While his body failed him in ways science has yet to understand. Never pretending to know how it felt to watch something that devastating happen, just raw support as I grappled with things I was ill-equipped to feel.

> There had been loss before my brother.
> I knew there would be loss after him.
> Life, it seemed, was more pain than joy.
> When you said: "Let's still be friends," you meant it.
> And when I needed a friend, there you were, ready with an embrace—no problem wiping away my tears with your bare hand.

WM

There are plenty of fish in the sea, yes, but some of those fish are more special than others. There are unseen heroes hiding among the hordes of squatters. Waiting for someone to figure them out, to pull at the frayed strings that bind them, allowing them soar.

I am certain of this.

X

X.

Say it out loud again twenty-five more times and you will understand.

Y

There are times when we want to quit. Where we ask ourselves, "Why bother?"

Z

ZS

Sometimes those "Yous" called me on it, sometimes they didn't. There were times when I called them on it, and times when I didn't.

Of course I tried to get away with little lies and half-truths when I felt they were necessary.

It is what it is.

But whenever someone said, "Be honest," I always found it hard not to be, thereafter. It could have been a sensitive conscience or a lack of confidence in my ability to lie with a straight face.

Either way.

"Be honest."

And the jig was up.

"Okay. Honestly, I've never been in love."

"I was in love once," you said. For a second you were more of a dreamer than me.

I was honest when I told you I had never been in love.

That was, of course, years ago.

Because in a dating alphabet Z can come before N and T can come after Z.

ZS

Honestly, I wasn't always listening.

Not just to you, but to everyone in general. It used to bother my parents the most, especially my father, who always thought more in lines than in colors. While I was busy daydreaming—which I did do often—I was more apt to forget the reminder he gave me to take out the garbage or cut the grass. He always thought it was an excuse when I said, "I forgot," or "I don't remember you saying that." But it wasn't an excuse, I had forgotten because I was elsewhere when he asked.

An errand or chore should always play second-fiddle to inspiration.

"It has to get done," he would say.

"Just do it first and then do whatever you want," my mother would add.

She understood more than he, but she, too, had her fiddles mixed up. It's perfectly fine for worlds to move at different speeds.

So when I pulled my head back out of the clouds to ask again, "How many siblings did you say you have?" and you had to repeat, "Four," it wasn't anything personal.

ZS

"It's windy out," you said.

So I removed my jacket and went to hand it to you, because—if I'm telling the truth—I've never minded the wind.

The wind can make you feel alive.

The wind can make you feel lots of things.

It can be the first warning sign of a looming storm.

Symbolize fear. Make you change your mind.

It can give a voice to the live green leaves in the trees or it can bully the dead brown ones on the ground.

"I don't want your jacket," you said. "I like to feel the wind."

"Me too," I said. "Me too."

So I set the jacket down on a park bench while we walked. The path, after all, circled back around so I knew we wouldn't be absent from it long.

It can give you goose bumps.

It can dry the sweat from your skin.

Hinder your sense of sound, yet enliven your sense of touch.

So you touched my arm and teased, "My, my…" fingering my goose bumps like one would reading brail.

"Look at the kites!" I said, excited.

I don't understand why but to me kites have always been a symbol of hope.

"Cute," you said, more or less referencing the little girl holding the string, missing the point.

So we walked on in the wind.

I, watching the kites, my head in the clouds, like always. And you, with your eyes more grounded, less hopeful, but also less likely to walk into a tree.

Finally the path began to repeat. But when we returned to the bench where I had left my jacket to rest, it was gone.

Like so many things are when we go back for them.

Acknowledgments

This, to me, is one of my favorite parts! As always, endless thanks to Kelly Smith for her guidance and patience. Thank you to John Martinetti of JEM Graphics for his hard work on the website and for encouraging me like no one else has. Thanks to Anthony Prasa, who amazes me by juggling so many different projects at once, for his help designing the book's cover. To my writer friends Rich Polk and Linda Rawlins, for taking time out of their busy schedules to help promote my work. To David Fulcher of Samsara literary magazine, for his kind words. Thanks to Matthew Kosinski, whose literary skills, constructive criticism, and advice are always appreciated. To Victor Alcindor, teacher, writer, and friend. To Mary Ann McGonigle for her wisdom and keen eye. To my friends at the Book Barn in Denville, NJ…especially Lenny, for running the best used book store there is. I am very fortunate to have many close friends, all of whom deserve recognition for their unconditional support. Thank you: Joseph Perna, Michael Paglucci, Michael Cohen, Joseph Trembley, Sean Clayton, Anthony Dietrick, Timothy Jonas, Paul Goskowski, Aj Koehnlein, Anthony Piserchio, Glen Coppola, Nick Abrantes, Brian Amorim, Brandi Brennan, Gina Piserchio, Aubrey DeNigris…you are all the best! Very special thanks to those who supported the Kickstarter campaign for this book: Chris & Mary Falkiewicz, Joe & Jen DeMeglio, Dave & Joelle Brownlee, Paul & Heather Barbato, Steven & Debi Molinaro, Joanne Barbato, Freddie Shivdat, Stephan Zichella, Anthony

Piserchio, and many others…your generosity is a blessing. Thank you to my sister Alaina, who gave me the pocket notebook that much of this story was originally written in, and for her advice after reading an early version of the book's manuscript. Thanks to my parents, Louis and Linda, for believing in me…and for everything. To the rest of my family and friends for their encouragement and love. To any writer who has ever inspired me in some small way. To you, the reader, who I hope found this story enjoyable and relatable. And finally, to all of the letters in my own Alphabet, who have unknowingly taught and given me so much.

Thank you all.

And now…a brief preview of
Joseph Anthony's new book:

Some College Somewhere

Stories chronicling the life of a self-destructive college student.

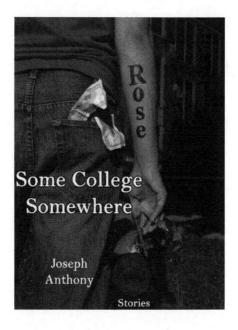

Available at → **diamondmillpress.com**

Reserve your copy today!

Aftermath, Beforemath

The blood in my veins feels as if it has been drained from me, spun in a centrifuge, purified, and returned to me while I slept. I can't remember returning to my apartment, but somehow I know where everything is. My arm reaches out with a mind of its own until my hand finds the water bottle it is seeking. It can be deciphered by the minimal amount of pain in my eyes that I have not slept with my contacts in. Rolling from my stomach to my back, it feels as if my neck has disintegrated and my head might have spun off onto the floor, had the pillow not been here to catch it.

The nightlife around The University is a playground for children who miss their childhood—for those who need to escape reality at all costs. Some of us do manage to escape, at least until we wake up and pain mingles in where feeling has ceased, while the room slowly keeps spinning—or stops spinning. Regret see-saws with sheer happiness as a conscious mind mixes with one that has escaped into oblivion, and minute by minute as you lie there debating whether or not to move, you remember pieces of the night. Or maybe you can't. Either way, most of us don't care because whatever happened, happened. And we know that there is nothing we can do to change it except close our eyes and go back to sleep.

At the foot of my bed there is an old brass chest, on which folded blankets are kept. I can tell that the sun is high because of the glare it casts off the chest and onto the far wall by my closet. The blankets are tangled around me. This time I did not make it under the comforter. I ball the blankets up, throw them down to my feet, and kick them onto the chest to end the glare. There is no point in folding them if I am going out again tonight. With the glare silenced, the sun reveals other things in the room. There are fingerprints in the dust on the blank TV screen, which stands on the tall dresser by the closet. Each fingerprint tells a story of a small action that has since been forgotten. Hands that had brushed up against its face by accident left more memorable traces than they may have known.

The shadow of giant wings darkens the floor. Turning to the windowsill, I see an orange butterfly with black spots pretending to be something much bigger than it really is. For a moment it has succeeded and I am moved by this phenomenon. How something so small can appear giant under the right circumstances. I stretch my legs, feeling hot, new, pain shoot from my ankle straight up to my hip. My jeans are hard and crackly by the knee and when I pull the material away from the leg itself, I can hear raw skin tearing from the dried blood. It is new skin, the skin that sits on top of a fresh wound, destroyed before it has the chance to harden and desensitize. Pain only lasts as long as it takes new skin to grow.

Alcohol is a wonderful thing, but painkillers—pain-assassins—are much more wonderful. They cut the leg off at the knee, temporarily, and replace the missing limb with a smile. ☺

All things in life are temporary. Pain, hopelessness, bliss, euphoria—all fleeting. You can hold onto nothing longer than you are meant to have it. Our greatest happinesses, our greatest anguishes, are gone before they are fully recognized. And, like fingerprints in the dust on a TV screen, all that they leave is an intricate imprint on our memories to be deciphered in their aftermath.

There's a mirror on the ceiling, so I stare at my reflection, wondering how the young man in the image can look so much like me. *Fuck you*, I say to him as I roll over, but nothing changes in the picture on the ceiling. I reach up for him and he reaches back, locked in a staring contest that both of us refuse to concede. My arm drops back to the bed, lactic acid dissipating in the cool bed sheets, but his arm remains outstretched and nothing could be stranger. He's amazing. *How do you do that?* I wish that he would answer. Smoke and mirrors clearly, as is all magic. I'm charmed by his smile. There is something genuine about it, while at the same time, something undeniably different from anything I've ever seen before. I ask him to marry me, but before he can answer, I break up with him. My heart is already taken.

It is? he asks.

Oh, yes.

I'm too late then?

Yes. Much too late. It's too late for you and me.

It's too late for you and me.

Shut up.

Shut up.

Fuck you.

Fuck you.

He goes back to sleep and is gone when I wake up.

Yesterday is the same as today and today is the same as tomorrow. There are beautiful prints of masterpieces by Rembrandt and Monet on the wall opposite my bed. These paintings were expensive, but I have enough money. I love to paint and to look at paintings—one of my only surviving passions—so they were worth it. Make no mind paying for something you love.

My phone is on the floor across the room in pieces below a painting of the ocean. *Impression Sunrise.* The screen is cracked like a mirror that has shattered and somehow managed to hold itself together. There is a hole in the sheetrock too misshapen to be from a fist. The necklace I am wearing is choking me, so I take hold of it and pull, breaking it into a thousand silver pieces. My feet are cold and the smell of my own body bothers me. Like a zombie, I roll out of bed. Begin stagger-walking to my phone with an urgency that I cannot explain. No one ever calls me. On my knees I pick up the pieces and with them clenched together between the dry lips of my mouth, I limp-crawl toward the bathroom.

As the water heats up, I stand and piss into the shower drain. The liquid leaving my body is yellow and dark. As I watch it dilute in the water and disappear, I sit on the edge of the tub with my dick in my hand, thinking for a while about things I cannot remember. Finally, the tub begins to look more and more like a comfortable bed. The hot water soaks my clothes. The steam begins to clear my nose and I am thankful for the deep, unlabored breaths. I put my phone back together while I lay in the tub, but it does not work, the battery must be dead. Ivy comes to mind and I am in Italy. Grape vines and wine—fine wine. I vomit and the darkness inside washes away, aided by the hot water. No one is more successful at navigating the aftermath than I am.

Today everything is the same as it was yesterday. Yesterday longs for tomorrow but can never catch it. I can never catch it.

There is only yesterday for me.

With everything left in me, I push my pants to my ankles. Oh, the sweet smell of ivy. Laughter takes a firm grip on my shoulders and shakes me hard. My head bangs repeatedly on the shower tiles. The ivy leaves turn white, beginning to resemble stars. Too many stars for any one person to look directly at for an extended period of time. My hand is sent on an errand to bring the bathmat between the tiles and my skull, but it never returns.

The shower curtain is missing, its absence is obvious. There is a warm, wet feeling between my legs that can only mean one thing. Looking down at the blanket shielding my body from the water, I find the shower curtain. Sometimes I surprise myself, a waterproof blanket in the shower. God only knows how long it has been since the last time I opened my eyes. The water is still running and the room is still spinning so nothing has changed. But something is different. I'm dehydrated and my leg begins to cramp. Suddenly, a phone starts ringing, but I am too tired to lift my arms and answer it.

"Hello."

It's not my phone. It's from the apartment next door. The walls are thin. They are thin and covered with tiny droplets of water, so I lick them. I lift my right hand to my face to brush the bangs away from my eyes. My tongue is willing to meet my hand halfway as I pull the shower curtain towards my mouth, funneling water to my dry tongue, licking it up like a homeless puppy until my leg feels better.

As I lean over the edge of the tub, I find the bathmat in my left hand. I release it and stand up slowly, removing the wet jeans from my ankles. All the while, the shower keeps running, the water beats down on my arms, awakening a numbness in every track mark.

My head is pounding. Bread, Tylenol, butter, and more water—much more water—will help. It is incredibly difficult to take fast steps toward the kitchen without falling down, but closing my eyes helps me keep balance. *Do not take more than 8 caplets in 24 hours…*I've memorized the label long ago and it may be the smartest thing I've ever done. Still, I've found that taking more than 8 in 24 hours is okay, but I do not recommend taking more than 4 at any one time. I pour what looks like 4 caplets into my hand, taking them down with cold water, but I start to second guess myself. I may have actually just taken 5. Or was it only 4?

I sit down on the kitchen floor with my back against the cabinet and debate this for a long time. Eventually, I decide that it's no big deal. The difference between 4 and 5 of anything really isn't that significant at all. It just means that they will need to wait for me a little longer than usual tonight, which they will gladly do. They need my money to fill their needles, to fill their glasses and red cups. Yesterday will pick up where it left off, and we can forget about everything else in the world again.

The sun is gone. I'm not sure how I feel as I stand up from the kitchen floor, but I'm convinced that Tylenol is one of man's most underrated creations. My mind is clear and I don't realize I am smiling until I pass a mirror. I blink. He blinks. I touch the scar on my face. He touches the scar on his face. Each move is exactly like my own, but as I recall the last hallucination, this is not always true.

> *I'm too late then?*
> *Yes. Much too late.*

The steps I need to take before going out again tonight are clear, calculated, and meaningful. Clean up, then reset the stage. The first step is collecting the pieces of the broken silver necklace. I would like to throw them out because it is easier, but they still have value. The pieces can be traded for pills, so I pick them up and place them in an empty prescription bottle. The next steps are replacing the shower curtain, which is easy, throwing the wet clothes in the hamper, which is also easy, and spackling the hole in the wall, which is only practical to do at the end of the week—because there will be more holes to fix tomorrow—and since it is not the end of the week, this is the easiest.

Follow these next steps exactly. Failing to properly carry out one of them could be fatal. Straying from a perfect routine is not recommended. I know that I can get drunk-Matthew or high-Matthew—or both Matthew's—through the return home. First, break the seal on two 16.9oz water bottles, taking one large sip out of each. If they are full when I scramble for them later, they will spill on my face. If they spill on my face, I may start to cough. If I start to cough, I may choke.

I take a new trash bag with handles, put it in the garbage bin, and place it down on the floor next to the water bottles at the side of the bed. The throw rug is already rolled up neatly under the window. If it is left out, it may be thrown up on or tripped over. I reach out and twist the blinds so that they are more open. Allowing some sunlight to come through in the morning is vital for waking up and starting the recovery process again. One of the most important things is throwing out the old contact solution and placing the contact case on my pillow so that I see it before crashing into bed. On more than one occasion I have lost lenses in my eyes while sleeping.

The most often forgotten step is turning the computer off and placing the battery and power cord as far away as possible. This is the one thing that fucked-up-Matthew will forget if I hide them well enough. I don't want to wind up on Facebook or the internet after I return…it's not a good situation. I don't need to worry about using Facebook on my phone because my own passcode will frustrate—stop me.

Finally, I take basketball shorts and an old t-shirt and lay them directly on the bed for easy access, just in case I'm coherent enough to change clothes, and I make sure to make the bed and fold a flap over so that I can see the sheets. This formula makes returning to the apartment as smooth as possible, as long as everything is done carefully and thoroughly beforehand.

My name is Matthew Rose. I was not always like this.

To stop caring about everything, you need to have once cared about something. There is peace in letting go, in giving in to the destruction. When there is nothing left to lose, there is nothing left to worry about. The moment I discovered this, a huge weight was lifted from me.

Not every man is meant to survive a sinking ship. While every man may have a right to live, not every man is capable of saving himself. That is why only a few people, a few workable parts, may be pulled from the great destruction of the Titanic, or the little destruction of my cell phone. The only thing I can salvage from the wreckage is the sim card. He is my refugee, and it is my job to find him a new home. I pick a box off the top of the stack of new phones in the corner of my closet, cut the tape away from the edges, and assemble the pieces with a mechanical precision that frightens me. Everything ends as it begins.

There is no exception to this.

Made in the USA
Middletown, DE
26 December 2016